THE SECRET GLORY

Arthur Machen

First published 2014
Copyright © 2014 Aziloth Books

This publication is designed to provide authoritative and accurate information in regard to the subject matter covered. It is sold on the understanding that the Publisher is not engaged in rendering professional services.

British Library Cataloguing in Publication Data

A catalogue record for this book is available from the British Library

ISBN-13: 978-1-909735-37-8

Printed and bound in Great Britain by Lightning Source UK Ltd., 6 Precedent Drive, Rooksley, Milton Keynes MK13 8PR.

Cover Illustration: *The Attainment* (Sir Galahad).
William Morris (C.1900)

CONTENTS

Note

One of the schoolmasters in "The Secret Glory" has views on
the subject of football similar to those entertained by a well-known
schoolmaster whose Biography appeared many years ago. That is
the only link between the villain of invention and the good man of
real life.

PREFACE

Some years ago I met my old master, Sir Frank Benson - he was Mr. F. R. Benson then - and he asked me in his friendly way what I had been doing lately.

"I am just finishing a book," I replied, "a book that everybody will hate."

"As usual," said the Don Quixote of our English stage - if I knew any nobler title to bestow upon him, I would, bestow it - "as usual; running your head against a stone wall!"

Well, I don't know about "as usual"; there may be something to be said for the personal criticism or there may not; but it has struck me that Sir Frank's remark is a very good description of "The Secret Glory," the book I had in mind as I talked to him. It is emphatically the history of an unfortunate fellow who ran his head against stone walls from the beginning to the end. He could think nothing and do nothing after the common fashion of the world; even when he "went wrong," he did so in a highly unusual and eccentric manner. It will be for the reader to determine whether he were a saint who had lost his way in the centuries or merely an undeveloped lunatic; I hold no passionate view on either side. In every age, there are people great and small for whom the times are out of joint, for whom everything is, somehow, wrong and askew. Consider Hamlet; an amiable man and an intelligent man. But what a mess he made of it! Fortunately, my hero - or idiot, which you will - was not called upon to intermeddle with affairs of State, and so only brought himself to grief: if it were grief; for the least chink of the door should be kept open, I am inclined to hold, for the other point of view. I have just been rereading Kipling's "The Miracle of Purun Bhagat," the tale of the Brahmin Prime Minister of the Native State in India, who saw all the world and the glory of it, in the West as well as in the East, and suddenly abjured all to become a hermit in the wood. Was he mad, or was he supremely wise? It is just a matter of opinion.

The origin and genesis of "The Secret Glory" were odd enough. Once on a time, I read the life of a famous schoolmaster, one of the most notable schoolmasters of these later days. I believe he was an excellent man in every way; but, somehow, that "Life" got on my nerves. I thought that the School Songs - for which, amongst other things, this master was famous - were drivel; I thought his views about football, regarded, not as a good game, but as the discipline and guide of life, were rot, and poisonous rot at that. In a word, the "Life" of this excellent man got my back up.

Very good. The year after, schoolmasters and football had ceased to engage my attention. I was deeply interested in a curious and minute investigation of the wonderful legend of the Holy Grail; or rather, in one aspect of that extraordinary complex. My researches led me to the connection of the Grail Legend with the vanished Celtic Church which held the field in Britain in the fifth and sixth and seventh centuries; I undertook an extraordinary and fascinating journey into a misty and uncertain region of Christian history. I must not say more here, lest - as Nurse says to the troublesome and persistent child - I "begin all over again"; but, indeed, it was a voyage on perilous seas, a journey to faery lands forlorn - and I would declare, by the way, my conviction that if there had been no Celtic Church, Keats could never have written those lines of tremendous evocation and incantation.

Again; very good. The year after, it came upon me to write a book. And I hit upon an original plan; or so I thought. I took my dislike of the good schoolmaster's "Life," I took my knowledge of Celtic mysteries - and combined my information.

Original, this plan! It was all thought of years before I was born. Do you remember the critic of the "Eatanswill Gazette"? He had to review for that admirable journal a work on Chinese Metaphysics. Mr. Pott tells the story of the article.

"He read up for the subject, at my desire, in the Encyclopædia Britannica ... he read for metaphysics under the letter M, and for China under the letter C, and combined his information!"

THE SECRET GLORY

CHAPTER I

I

A heavy cloud passed swiftly away before the wind that came with the night, and far in a clear sky the evening star shone with pure brightness, a gleaming world set high above the dark earth and the black shadows in the lane. In the ending of October a great storm had blown from the west, and it was through the bare boughs of a twisted oak that Ambrose Meyrick saw the silver light of the star. As the last faint flash died in the sky he leaned against a gate and gazed upward; and then his eyes fell on the dull and weary undulations of the land, the vast circle of dun ploughland and grey meadow bounded by a dim horizon, dreary as a prison wall. He remembered with a start how late it must be; he should have been back an hour before, and he was still in the open country, a mile away at least from the outskirts of Lupton. He turned from the star and began to walk as quickly as he could along the lane through the puddles and the sticky clay, soaked with three weeks' heavy rain.

He saw at last the faint lamps of the nearest streets where the shoemakers lived and he tramped hurriedly through this wretched quarter, past its penny shops, its raw public-house, its rawer chapel, with twelve foundation-stones on which are written the names of the twelve leading Congregationalists of Lupton, past the squalling children whose mothers were raiding and harrying them to bed. Then came the Free Library, an admirable instance, as the *Lupton Mercury* declared, of the adaptation of Gothic to modern requirements. From a sort of tower of this building a great arm shot out and hung a round clock-face over the street, and Meyrick experienced another shock when he saw that it was even later than he had feared. He had to get to the other side of the town, and it was past seven already! He began to run, wondering what his fate would be at his uncle's hands, and he went by "our grand old parish church" (completely "restored" in the early 'forties), past the remains of the market-cross, converted most successfully, according to local opinion, into a drinking fountain for dogs and cattle, dodging his way among the late shoppers and the early loafers who lounged to and fro along the High Street.

He shuddered as he rang the bell at the Old Grange. He tried to put a bold face on it when the servant opened the door, and he would have gone straight down the hall into the schoolroom, but the girl stopped him.

"Master said you're to go to the study at once, Master Meyrick, as soon as ever you come in."

She was looking strangely at him, and the boy grew sick with dread. He was a "funk" through and through, and was frightened out of his wits about twelve times a day every day of his life. His uncle had said a few years before: "Lupton will make a man of you," and Lupton was doing its best. The face of the miserable wretch whitened and grew wet; there was a choking sensation in his throat, and he felt very cold. Nelly Foran, the maid, still looked at him with strange, eager eyes, then whispered suddenly:

"You must go directly, Master Meyrick, Master heard the bell, I know; but I'll make it up to you."

Ambrose understood nothing except the approach of doom. He drew a long breath and knocked at the study door, and entered on his uncle's command.

It was an extremely comfortable room. The red curtains were drawn close, shutting out the dreary night, and there was a great fire of coal that bubbled unctuously and shot out great jets of flame - in the schoolroom they used coke. The carpet was soft to the feet, and the chairs promised softness to the body, and the walls were well furnished with books. There were Thackeray, Dickens, Lord Lytton, uniform in red morocco, gilt extra; the Cambridge Bible for Students in many volumes, Stanley's *Life of Arnold*, Coplestone's *Prælectiones Academicæ*, commentaries, dictionaries, first editions of Tennyson, school and college prizes in calf, and, of course, a great brigade of Latin and Greek classics. Three of the wonderful and terrible pictures of Piranesi hung in the room; these Mr.

Horbury admired more for the subject-matter than for the treatment, in which he found, as he said, a certain lack of the *aurea mediocritas* - almost, indeed, a touch of morbidity. The gas was turned low, for the High Usher was writing at his desk, and a shaded lamp cast a bright circle of light on a mass of papers.

He turned round as Ambrose Meyrick came in. He had a high, bald forehead, and his fresh-coloured face was edged with reddish "mutton-chop" whiskers. There was a dangerous glint in his grey-green eyes, and his opening sentence was unpromising.

"Now, Ambrose, you must understand quite definitely that this sort of thing is not going to be tolerated any longer."

Perhaps it would not have fared quite so badly with the unhappy lad if only his uncle had not lunched with the Head. There was a concatenation accordingly, every link in which had helped to make Ambrose Meyrick's position hopeless. In the first place there was boiled mutton for luncheon, and this was a dish hateful to Mr. Horbury's palate. Secondly, the wine was sherry. Of this Mr. Horbury was very fond, but unfortunately the Head's sherry, though making a specious appeal to the taste, was in reality far from good and teemed with those fiery and irritating spirits which make the liver to burn and rage. Then Chesson had practically found fault with his chief assistant's work. He had not, of course, told him in so many words that he was unable to teach; he had merely remarked:

"I don't know whether you've noticed it, Horbury, but it struck me the other day that there was a certain lack of grip about those fellows of yours in the fifth. Some of them struck me as *muddlers*, if you know what I mean: there was a

9

sort of *vagueness*, for example, about their construing in that chorus. Have you remarked anything of the kind yourself?"

And then, again, the Head had gone on:

"And, by the way, Horbury, I don't quite know what to make of your nephew, Meyrick. He was your wife's nephew, wasn't he? Yes. Well, I hardly know whether I can explain what I feel about the boy; but I can't help saying that there is something wrong about him. His work strikes me as good enough - in fact, quite above the form average - but, to use the musical term, he seems to be in the wrong key. Of course, it may be my fancy; but the lad reminds me of those very objectionable persons who are said to have a joke up their sleeve. I doubt whether he is taking the Lupton stamp; and when he gets up in the school I shall be afraid of his influence on the other boys."

Here, again, the master detected a note of blame; and by the time he reached the Old Grange he was in an evil humour. He hardly knew which he found the more offensive - Chesson's dish or his discourse. He was a dainty man in his feeding, and the thought of the great fat gigot pouring out a thin red stream from the gaping wound dealt to it by the Head mingled with his resentment of the indirect scolding which he considered that he had received, and on the fire just kindled every drop of that corrosive sherry was oil. He drank his tea in black silence, his rage growing fiercer for want of vent, and it is doubtful whether in his inmost heart he was altogether displeased when report was made at six o'clock that Meyrick had not come in. He saw a prospect - more than a prospect - of satisfactory relief.

Some philosophers have affirmed that lunatic doctors (or mental specialists) grow in time to a certain resemblance to their patients, or, in more direct language, become half mad themselves. There seems a good deal to be said for the position; indeed, it is probably a more noxious madness to swear a man into perpetual imprisonment in the company of maniacs and imbeciles because he sings in his bath and will wear a purple dressing-gown at dinner than to fancy oneself Emperor of China. However this may be, it is very certain that in many cases the schoolmaster is nothing more or less than a bloated schoolboy: the beasts are, radically, the same, but morbid conditions have increased the venom of the former's sting. Indeed, it is not uncommon for well-wishers to the great Public School System to praise their favourite masters in terms which admit, nay, glory in, this identity. Read the memorial tributes to departed Heads in a well-known and most respectable Church paper. "To the last he was a big boy at heart," writes Canon Diver of his friend, that illiterate old sycophant who brought up the numbers of the school to such a pitch by means of his conciliator policy to Jews, Turks, heretics and infidels that there was nothing for it but to make him a bishop. "I always thought he seemed more at home in the playing fields than in the sixth-form room.... He had all the English boy's healthy horror of anything approaching pose or eccentricity.... He could be a severe disciplinarian when severity seemed necessary, but everybody in the school knew that a well-placed 'boundary,' a difficult catch or a goal well won or well averted would atone for all but the most serious offences." There are many other points of resemblance between the average master and the average boy: each, for example, is intensely cruel, and experiences a quite abnormal joy in the infliction of pain. The baser boy tortures those animals which are not *méchants*. Tales have been told (they are hushed up by all true friends of the "System") of wonderful and exquisite orgies in lonely hollows of the moors, in obscure and hidden thickets: tales of a boy or two, a lizard or a toad, and the slow simmering heat of a bonfire. But these are the exceptional pleasures of the *virtuosi*; for the average lad there is plenty of fun to be got out of his feebler fellows, of whom there are generally a few even in the healthiest community. After all, the weakest must go to the wall, and if the bones of the weakest are ground in the process, that is their fault. When some miserable little wretch, after a year or two of prolonged and exquisite torture of body and mind, seeks the last escape of suicide, one knows how the Old Boys will come forward, how gallantly they will declare that the days at the "dear old school" were the happiest in their lives; how "the Doctor" was their father and the Sixth their nursing-mother; how the delights of the Mahomedans' fabled Paradise are but grey and weary sport compared with the joys of the happy fag, whose heart, as the inspired bard of Harrow tells us, will thrill in future years at the thought of the Hill. They write from all quarters, these brave Old Boys: from the hard-won Deanery, result of many years of indefatigable attack on the fundamental doctrines of the Christian faith; from the comfortable villa, the reward of commercial activity and acuteness on the Stock Exchange; from the courts and from the camps; from all the high seats of the successful; and common to them all is the convincing argument of praise. And we all agree, and say there is nothing like our great Public Schools, and perhaps the only dissentient voices are those of the father and mother who bury the body of a little child about whose neck is the black sign of the rope. But let them be comforted: the boy was no good at games, though his torments were not bad sport while he lasted.

Mr. Horbury was an old Luptonian; he was, in the words of Canon Diver, but "a big boy at heart," and so he gave orders that Meyrick was to be sent in the study directly he came in, and he looked at the clock on the desk before him with satisfaction and yet with impatience. A hungry man may long for his delayed dinner almost with a sense of fury, and yet at the back of his mind he cannot help being consoled by the thought of how wonderfully he will enjoy the soup when it appears at last. When seven struck, Mr. Horbury moistened his lips slightly. He got up and felt cautiously behind one of the bookshelves. The object was there, and he sat down again. He listened; there were footfalls on the drive. Ah! there was the expected ring. There was a brief interval, and then a knock. The fire was glowing with red flashes, and the wretched toad was secured.

"Now, Ambrose, you must understand quite definitely that this sort of thing isn't going to be tolerated any longer. This is the third time during this term that you have been late for lockup. You know the rules: six o'clock at latest. It is now twenty minutes past seven. What excuse have you to make? What have you been doing with yourself? Have you been in the Fields?"

"No, Sir."

"Why not? You must have seen the Resolution of the Sixth on the notice-board of the High School? You know what it promised any boy who shirked rocker? 'A good sound thrashing with tuds before the First Thirty.' I am afraid you will have a very bad time of it on Monday, after Graham has sent up your name to the Room."

There was a pause. Mr. Horbury looked quietly and lengthily at the boy, who stood white and sick before him. He was a rather sallow, ugly lad of fifteen. There was something of intelligence in his expression, and it was this glance that Chesson, the Headmaster, had resented. His heart beat against his breast, his breath came in gasps and the sweat of terror poured down his body. The master gazed at him, and at last spoke again.

"But what have you been doing? Where have you been all this time?"

"If you please, Sir, I walked over to Selden Abbey."

"To Selden Abbey? Why, it's at least six miles away! What on earth did you want to go to Selden Abbey for? Are you fond of old stones?"

"If you please, Sir, I wanted to see the Norman arches. There is a picture of them in *Parker's Glossary*."

"Oh, I see! You are a budding antiquarian, are you, Ambrose, with an interest in Norman arches - eh? I suppose we are to look forward to the time when your researches will have made Lupton famous? Perhaps you would like to lecture to the school on St. Paul's Cathedral? Pray, what are your views as to the age of Stonehenge?"

The wit was heavy enough, but the speaker's position gave a bitter sting to his lash. Mr. Horbury saw that every cut had told, and, without prejudice to more immediate and acuter pleasures, he resolved that such biting satire must have a larger audience. Indeed, it was a long time before Ambrose Meyrick heard the last of those wretched Norman arches. The method was absurdly easy. "Openings" presented themselves every day. For example, if the boy made a mistake in construing, the retort was obvious:

"Thank you, Meyrick, for your most original ideas on the force of the aorist. Perhaps if you studied your Greek Grammar a little more and your favourite *Glossary of Architecture* a little less, it would be the better. Write out 'Aorist means indefinite' five hundred times."

Or, again, perhaps the Classic Orders were referred to. Mr. Horbury would begin to instruct the form as to the difference between Ionic and Doric. The form listened with poor imitation of interest. Suddenly the master would break off:

"I beg your pardon. I was forgetting that we have a great architectural authority amongst us. Be so kind as to instruct us, Meyrick. What does Parker say? Or perhaps you have excogitated some theories of your own? I know you have an original mind, from the extraordinary quantities of your last copy of verse. By the way, I must ask you to write out 'The *e* in *venio* is short' five hundred times. I am sorry to interfere with your more important architectural studies, but I am afraid there is no help for it."

And so on; while the form howled with amusement.

But Mr. Horbury kept these gems for future and public use. For the moment he had more exciting work on hand. He burst out suddenly:

"The fact is, Ambrose Meyrick, you're a miserable little humbug! You haven't the honesty to say, fair and square, that you funked rocker and went loafing about the country, looking for any mischief you could lay your hands on. Instead of that you make up this cock-and-bull story of Selden Abbey and Norman arches - as if any boy in his senses ever knew or cared twopence about such things! I hope you haven't been spending the afternoon in some low public-house? There, don't speak! I don't want to hear any more lies. But, whatever you have been doing, you have broken the rules, and you must be taught that the rules have to be kept. Stand still!"

Mr. Horbury went to the bookshelf and drew out the object. He stood at a little distance behind Meyrick and opened proceedings with a savage cut at his right arm, well above the elbow. Then it was the turn of the left arm, and the master felt the cane bite so pleasantly into the flesh that he distributed some dozen cuts between the two arms. Then he turned his attention to the lad's thighs and finished up in the orthodox manner, Meyrick bending over a chair.

The boy's whole body was one mass of burning, stinging torture; and, though he had not uttered a sound during the process, the tears were streaming down his cheeks. It was not the bodily anguish, though that was extreme enough, so much as a far-off recollection. He was quite a little boy, and his father, dead long since, was showing him the western doorway of a grey church on a high hill and carefully instructing him in the difference between "billetty" and "chevronny."

"It's no good snivelling, you know, Ambrose. I daresay you think me severe, but, though you won't believe me now, the day will come when you will thank me from your heart for what I have just done. Let this day be a turning-point in your life. Now go to your work."

II

It was strange, but Meyrick never came in the after days and thanked his uncle for that sharp dose of physical and mental pain. Even when he was a man he dreamed of Mr. Horbury and woke up in a cold sweat, and then would fall asleep again with a great sigh of relief and gladness as he realised that he was no longer in the power of that "infernal old swine," "that filthy, canting, cruel brute," as he roughly called his old master.

The fact was, as some old Luptonians remarked, the two had never understood one another. With the majority of the boys the High Usher passed for a popular master enough. He had been a distinguished athlete in his time, and up to his last days at the school was a football enthusiast. Indeed, he organised a variety of the Lupton game which met with immense popularity till the Head was reluctantly compelled to stop it; some said because he always liked to drop bitter into Horbury's cup when possible; others - and with more probability on their side - maintained that it was in consequence of a report received from the school doctor to the effect that this new species of football was rapidly setting up an old species of heart disease in the weaker players.

However that might be, there could be no doubt as to Horbury's intense and deep-rooted devotion to the school. His father had been a Luptonian before him. He himself had gone from the school to the University, and within a year or two of taking his degree he had returned to Lupton to serve it as a master. It was the general opinion in Public School circles that the High Usher had counted for as much as Chesson, the Headmaster, if not for more, in the immense advance in prestige and popularity that the school had made; and everybody thought that when Chesson received the episcopal order Horbury's succession was a certainty. Unfortunately, however, there were wheels within wheels, and a total stranger was appointed, a man who knew nothing of the famous Lupton traditions, who (it was whispered) had been heard to say that "this athletic business" was getting a bit overdone. Mr. Horbury's friends were furious, and Horbury himself, it was supposed, was bitterly disappointed. He retreated to one of the few decent canonries which have survived the wave of agricultural depression; but those who knew him best doubted whether his ecclesiastical duties were an adequate consolation for the loss of that coveted Headmastership of Lupton.

To quote the memoir which appeared in the *Guardian* soon after his death, over some well-known initials:

"His friends were shocked when they saw him at the Residence. He seemed no longer the same man, he had aged more in six months, as some of them expressed themselves, than in the dozen years before. The old joyous Horbury, full of mirth, an apt master of word-play and logic-fence, was somehow 'dimmed,' to use the happy phrase of a former colleague, the Dean of Dorchester. Old Boys who remembered the sparkle of his wit, the zest which he threw into everything, making the most ordinary form-work better fun than the games at other schools, as one of them observed, missed something indefinable from the man whom they had loved so long and so well. One of them, who had perhaps penetrated as closely as any into the *arcana* of Horbury's friendship (a privilege which he will ever esteem as one of the greatest blessings of his life), tried to rouse him with an extravagant rumour which was then going the round of the popular Press, to the effect that considerable modifications were about to be introduced into the compulsory system of games at X., one of the greatest of our great Public Schools. Horbury flushed; the old light came into his eyes; his friend was reminded of the ancient war-horse who hears once more the inspiring notes of the trumpet. 'I can't believe it,' he said, and there was a tremor in his voice. 'They wouldn't dare. Not even Y. (the Headmaster of X.) would do such a scoundrelly thing as that. I won't believe it.' But the flush soon faded and his apathy returned. 'After all,' he said, 'I shouldn't wonder if it were so. Our day is past, I suppose, and for all I know they may be construing the Breviary and playing dominoes at X. in a few years' time.'

"I am afraid that those last years at Wareham were far from happy. He felt, I think, out of tune with his surroundings, and, *pace* the readers of the Guardian, I doubt whether he was ever quite at home in his stall. He confessed to one of his old associates that he doubted the wisdom of the whole Cathedral system. 'What,' he said, in his old characteristic manner, 'would St. Peter say if he could enter this building and see that gorgeous window in which he is represented with mitre, cope and keys?' And I do not think that he was ever quite reconciled to the daily recitation of the Liturgy, accompanied as it is in such establishments by elaborate music and all the pomp of the surpliced choir. 'Rome and water, Rome and water!' he has been heard to mutter under his breath as the procession swept up the nave, and before he died I think that he had the satisfaction of feeling that many in high places were coming round to his views.

"But to the very last he never forgot Lupton. A year or two before he died he wrote the great school song, 'Follow, follow, follow!' He was pleased, I know, when it appeared in the *Luptonian*, and a famous Old Boy informs me that he will never forget Horbury's delight when he was told that the song was already a great favourite in 'Chantry.' To many of your readers the words will be familiar; but I cannot resist quoting the first verse:

> "I am getting old and grey and the hills seem far away,
> And I cannot hear the horn that once proclaimed the morn
> When we sallied forth upon the chase together;
> For the years are gone - alack! - when we hastened on the track,
> And the huntsman's whip went crack! as a signal to our pack
> Riding in the sunshine and fair weather.
> And yet across the ground
> I seem to hear a sound,
> A sound that comes up floating from the hollow;
> And its note is very clear As it echoes in my ear,
> And the words are: 'Lupton, follow, follow, follow!'

Chorus.

> *"Lupton, follow away!*
> *The darkness lies behind us, and before us is the day.*
> *Follow, follow the sun,*
> *The whole world's to be won,*
> *So, Lupton, follow, follow, follow, follow away!*

"An old pupil sang this verse to him on his death-bed, and I think, perhaps, that some at least of the readers of the Guardian will allow that George Horbury died 'fortified,' in the truest sense, 'with the rites of the Church' - the Church of a Great Aspiration."

Such was the impression that Mr. Horbury had evidently made upon some of his oldest friends; but Meyrick was, to the last, an infidel. He read the verses in the *Guardian* (he would never subscribe to the Luptonian) and jeered savagely at the whole sentiment of the memoir, and at the poetry, too.

"Isn't it incredible?" he would say. "Let's allow that the main purpose of the great Public Schools is to breed brave average boobies by means of rocker, sticker and mucker and the rest of it. Still, they do acknowledge that they have a sort of *parergon* - the teaching of two great literatures, two literatures that have moulded the whole of Western thought for more than two thousand years. And they pay an animal like this to teach these literatures - a swine that has not enough literature of any kind in him to save the soul of a louse! Look at those verses! Why, a decent fourth form boy would be ashamed to put his name to them!"

He was foolish to talk in this fashion. People merely said that it was evident he was one of the failures of the great Public School system; and the song was much admired in the right circles. A very well-turned *idem Latine* appeared in the *Guardian* shortly after the publication of the memoir, and the initials at the foot of the version were recognised as those of a literary dean.

And on that autumn evening, far away in the 'seventies, Meyrick, the boy, left Mr. Horbury's study in a white fury of grief and pain and rage. He would have murdered his master without the faintest compunction, nay, with huge delight. Psychologically, his frame of mind was quite interesting, though he was only a schoolboy who had just had a sound thrashing for breaking rules.

For the fact, of course, was that Horbury, the irritating influence of the Head's conversation and sherry apart, was by no means a bad fellow. He was for the moment savagely cruel, but then, most men are apt to be savagely cruel when they suffer from an inflamed liver and offensive superiors, more especially when there is an inferior, warranted defenceless, in their power. But, in the main, Horbury was a very decent specimen of his class - English schoolmaster - and Meyrick would never allow that. In all his reasoning about schools and schoolmasters there was a fatal flaw - he blamed both for not being what they never pretended to be. To use a figure that would have appealed to him, it was if one quarrelled with a plain, old-fashioned meeting-house because it was not in the least like Lincoln Cathedral. A chimney may not be a decorative object, but then it does not profess to be a spire or a pinnacle far in the spiritual city.

But Meyrick was always scolding meeting-houses because they were not cathedrals. He has been heard to rave for hours against useful, unpretentious chimney-pots because they bore no resemblance to celestial spires. Somehow or other, possibly by inheritance, possibly by the influence of his father's companionship, he had unconsciously acquired a theory of life which bore no relation whatever to the facts of it. The theory was manifest in his later years; but it must have been stubbornly, if vaguely, present in him all through his boyhood. Take, for instance, his comment on poor Canon Horbury's verses. He judged those, as we have seen, by the rules of the fine art of literature, and found them rubbish. Yet any old Luptonian would have told him that to hear the whole six hundred boys join in the chorus, "Lupton, follow away!" was one of the great experiences of life; from which it appears that the song, whatever its demerits from a literary point of view, fully satisfied the purpose for which is was written. In other words, it was an excellent chimney, but Meyrick still persisted in his easy and futile task of proving that it was not a bit like a spire. Then, again, one finds a fallacy of still huger extent in that major premiss of his: that the great Public Schools purpose to themselves as a secondary and minor object the imparting of the spirit and beauty of the Greek and Latin literatures. Now, it is very possible that at some distant period in the past this was an object, or even, perhaps, the object of the institutions in question. The Humanists, it may be conjectured, thought of school and University as places where Latin and Greek were to be learned, and to be learned with the object of enjoying the great thought and the great style of an antique world. One sees the spirit of this in Rabelais, for example. The Classics are a wonderful adventure; to learn to understand them is to be a spiritual Columbus, a discoverer of new seas and unknown continents, a drinker of new-old wine in a new-old land. To the student of those days a mysterious drowned Atlantis again rose splendid from the waves of the great deep. It was these things that Meyrick (unconsciously, doubtless) expected to find in his school life; it was for the absence of these things that he continued to scold the system in his later years; wherein, like Jim in *Huckleberry Finn*, he missed the point by a thousand miles.

The Latin and Greek of modern instruction are, of course, most curious and interesting survivals; no longer taught with any view of enabling students to enjoy and understand either the thought or beauty of the originals; taught rather in such a manner as to nauseate the learner for the rest of his days with the very notion of these lessons. Still, the study of the Classics survives, a curious and elaborate ritual, from which all sense and spirit have departed. One has only to recollect the form master's lessons in the *Odyssey* or the *Bacchæ*, and then to view modern Free-masons celebrating the Mystic Death and Resurrection of Hiram Abiff; the analogy is complete, for neither the master nor the Masons have the remotest notion of what they are doing. Both persevere in strange and mysterious actions from inveterate conservatism.

Meyrick was a lover of antiquity and a special lover of survivals, but he could never see that the round of Greek syntax, and Latin prose, of Elegiacs and verbs in Greek, with the mystery of the Oratio obliqua and the Optative, was one of the most strange and picturesque survivals of modern life. It is to be noted, by the way, that the very meaning of the word "scholar" has been radically changed. Thus a well-known authority points out that "Melancholy" Burton had no "scholarship" in the real sense of the word; he merely used his vast knowledge of ancient and modern literature to make one of the most entertaining and curious books that the world possesses. True "scholarship," in the modern sense, is to be sought for not in the Jacobean translators of the Bible, but in the Victorian revisers. The former made the greatest of English books out of their Hebrew and Greek originals; but the latter understood the force of the aorist. It is curious to reflect that "scholar" once meant a man of literary taste and knowledge.

Meyrick never mastered these distinctions, or, if he did so in later years, he never confessed to his enlightenment, but went on railing at the meeting-house, which, he still maintained, *did* pretend to be a cathedral. He has been heard to wonder why a certain Dean, who had pointed out the vast improvements that had been effected by the Revisers, did not employ a few young art students from Kensington to correct the infamous drawing of the fourteenth-century glass in his cathedral. He was incorrigible; he was always incorrigible, and thus, in his boyhood, on the dark November evening, he meditated the murder of his good master and uncle - for at least a quarter of an hour.

His father, he remembered, had always spoken of Gothic architecture as the most wonderful and beautiful thing in the world: a thing to be studied and loved and reverenced. His father had never so much as mentioned rocker, much less had he preached it as the one way by which an English boy must be saved. Hence, Ambrose maintained inwardly that his visit to Selden Abbey was deserving of reward rather than punishment, and he resented bitterly, the savage injustice (as he thought it) of his caning.

III

Yet Mr. Horbury had been right in one matter, if not in all. That evening was a turning-point in Meyrick's life. He had felt the utmost rage of the enemy, as it were, and he determined that he would be a funk no longer. He would not degenerate into the state of little Phipps, who had been bullied and "rockered" and beaten into such a deplorable condition that he fainted dead away while the Headmaster was operating on him for "systematic and deliberate lying." Phipps not only fainted, but, being fundamentally sensible, as Dr. Johnson expressed it, showed a strong disinclination to return to consciousness and the precious balms of the "dear old Head." Chesson was rather frightened, and the school doctor, who had his living to get, said, somewhat dryly, that he thought the lad had better go home for a week or two.

So Phipps went home in a state which made his mother cry bitterly and his father wonder whether the Public School system was not over-praised. But the old family doctor went about raging and swearing at the "scoundrels" who had reduced a child of twelve to a nervous wreck, with "neurasthenia cerebralis" well on its way. But Dr. Walford had got his education in some trumpery little academy, and did not understand or value the *ethos* of the great Public Schools.

Now, Ambrose Meyrick had marked the career of wretched Phipps with concern and pity. The miserable little creature had been brought by careful handling from masters and boys to such a pitch of neurotic perfection that it was only necessary to tap him smartly on the back or on the arm, and he would instantly burst into tears. Whenever anyone asked him the simplest question he suspected a cruel trap of some sort, and lied and equivocated and shuffled with a pitiable lack of skill. Though he was pitched by the heels into mucker about three times a week, that he might acquire the useful art of natation, he still seemed to grow dirtier and dirtier. His school books were torn to bits, his exercises made into darts; he had impositions for losing books and canings for not doing his work, and he lied and cried all the more.

Meyrick had never got to this depth. He was a sturdy boy, and Phipps had always been a weakly little animal; but, as he walked from the study to the schoolroom after his thrashing, he felt that he had been in some danger of descending on that sad way. He finally resolved that he would never tread it, and so he walked past the baize-lined doors into the room where the other boys were at work on prep, with an air of unconcern which was not in the least assumed.

Mr. Horbury was a man of considerable private means and did not care to be bothered with the troubles and responsibilities of a big House. But there was room and to spare in the Old Grange, so he took three boys besides his nephew. These three were waiting with a grin of anticipation, since the nature of Meyrick's interview with "old Horbury" was not dubious. But Ambrose strolled in with a "Hallo, you fellows!" and sat down in his place as if nothing had happened. This was intolerable.

"I say, Meyrick," began Pelly, a beefy boy with a red face, "you *have* been blubbing! Feel like writing home about it? Oh! I forgot. This is your home, isn't it? How many cuts? I didn't hear you howl."

The boy took no notice. He was getting out his books as if no one had spoken.

"Can't you answer?" went on the beefy one. "How many cuts, you young sneak?"

"Go to hell!"

The whole three stared aghast for a moment; they thought Meyrick must have gone mad. Only one, Bates the observant, began to chuckle quietly to himself, for he did not like Pelly. He who was always beefy became beefier; his eyes bulged out with fury.

"I'll give it you," he said and made for Ambrose, who was turning over the leaves of the Latin dictionary. Ambrose did not wait for the assault; he rose also and met Pelly half-way with a furious blow, well planted on the nose. Pelly took a back somersault and fell with a crash to the floor, where he lay for a moment half stunned. He rose staggering and looked about him with a pathetic, bewildered air; for, indeed, a great part of his little world had crumbled about his ears. He stood in the middle of the room, wondering what it meant, whether it was true indeed that Meyrick was no longer of any use for a little quiet fun. A horrible and incredible transmutation had, apparently, been effected in the funk of old. Pelly gazed wildly about him as he tried to staunch the blood that poured over his mouth.

"Foul blow!" ventured Rawson, a lean lad who liked to twist the arms of very little boys till they shrieked for mercy. The full inwardness of the incident had not penetrated to his brain; he saw without believing, in the manner of the materialist who denies the marvellous even when it is before his eyes.

"Foul blow, young Meyrick!"

The quiet student had gone back to his place and was again handling his dictionary. It was a hard, compact volume, rebound in strong boards, and the edge of these boards caught the unfortunate Rawson full across the eyes with extraordinary force. He put his face in his hands and blubbered quietly and dismally, rocking to and fro in his seat, hardly hearing the fluent stream of curses with which the quiet student inquired whether the blow he had just had was good enough for him.

Meyrick picked up his dictionary with a volley of remarks which would have done credit to an old-fashioned stage-manager at the last dress rehearsal before production.

"Hark at him," said Pelly feebly, almost reverently. "Hark at him." But poor Rawson, rocking to and fro, his head between his hands, went on blubbering softly and spoke no word.

Meyrick had never been an unobservant lad; he had simply made a discovery that evening that in Rome certain Roman customs must be adopted. The wise Bates went on doing his copy of Latin verse, chuckling gently to himself. Bates was a cynic. He despised all the customs and manners of the place most heartily and took the most curious care to observe them. He might have been the inventor and patentee of rocker, if one judged him by the fervour with which he played it. He entered his name for every possible event at the sports, and jumped the jumps and threw the hammer and ran the races as if his life depended on it. Once Mr. Horbury had accidentally over-head Bates saying something about "the honour

20

of the House" which went to his heart. As for cricket, Bates played as if his sole ambition was to become a first-class professional. And he chuckled as he did his Latin verses, which he wrote (to the awe of other boys) "as if he were writing a letter" - that is, without making a rough copy. For Bates had got the "hang" of the whole system from rocker to Latin verse, and his copies were much admired. He grinned that evening, partly at the transmutation of Meyrick and partly at the line he was jotting down:

"Mira loquor, cœlo resonans vox funditur alto."

In after life he jotted down a couple of novels which sold, as the journalists said, "like hot cakes." Meyrick went to see him soon after the first novel had gone into its thirtieth thousand, and Bates was reading "appreciations" and fingering a cheque and chuckling.

"Mira loquor, populo, resonans, cheque funditur alto," he said. "I know what schoolmasters and boys and the public want, and I take care they get it - *sale espèce de sacrés cochons de N. de D.!"*

The rest of prep. went off quite quietly. Pelly was slowly recovering from the shock that he had received and began to meditate revenge. Meyrick had got him unawares, he reflected. It was merely an accident, and he resolved to challenge Meyrick to fight and give him back the worst licking he had ever had in his life. He was beefy, but a bold fellow. Rawson, who was really a cruel coward and a sneak, had made up his mind that he wanted no more, and from time to time cast meek and propitiatory glances in Meyrick's direction.

At half-past nine they all went into their dining-room for bread and cheese and beer. At a quarter to ten Mr. Horbury appeared in cap and gown and read a chapter from St. Paul's Epistle to the Romans, with one or two singularly maundering and unhappy prayers. He stopped the boys as they were going up to their rooms.

"What's this, Pelly?" he said. "Your nose is all swollen. It's been bleeding, too, I see. What have you been doing to yourself? And you, Rawson, how do you account for your eyes being black? What's the meaning of all this?"

"Please, Sir, there was a very stiff bully down at rocker this afternoon, and Rawson and I got tokered badly."

"Were you in the bully, Bates?"

"No, Sir; I've been outside since the beginning of the term. But all the fellows were playing up tremendously, and I saw Rawson and Pelly had been touched when we were changing."

"Ah! I see. I'm very glad to find the House plays up so well. As for you, Bates, I hear you're the best outside for your age that we've ever had. Good night."

The three said "Thank you, Sir," as if their dearest wish had been gratified, and the master could have sworn that Bates flushed with pleasure at his word of praise. But the fact was that Bates had "suggested" the flush by a cunning arrangement of his features.

The boys vanished and Mr. Horbury returned to his desk. He was editing a selection called "English Literature for Lower Forms." He began to read from the slips that he had prepared:

> *"So all day long the noise of battle roll'd*
> *Among the mountains by the winter sea;*
> *Until King Arthur's table, man by man,*
> *Had fallen in Lyonnesse - - "*

He stopped and set a figure by the last word, and then, on a blank slip, with a corresponding letter, he repeated the figure and wrote the note:

Lyonnesse - the Sicilly Isles.

Then he took a third slip and wrote the question:

Give the ancient name of the Sicilly Isles.

These serious labours employed him till twelve o'clock. He put the materials of his book away as the clock struck, and solemnly mixed himself his nightly glass of whisky and soda - in the daytime he never touched spirits - and bit the one cigar which he smoked in the twenty-four hours. The stings of the Head's sherry and of his conversation no longer burned within him; time and work and the bite of the cane in Meyrick's flesh had soothed his soul, and he set himself to dream, leaning back in his arm-chair, watching the cheerful fire.

He was thinking of what he would do when he succeeded to the Headmastership. Already there were rumours that Chesson had refused the Bishopric of St. Dubric's in order that he might be free to accept Dorchester, which, in the nature of things, must soon be vacant. Horbury had no doubt that the Headmastership would be his; he had influential friends who assured him that the trustees would not hesitate for an instant. Then he would show the world what an English Public School could be made. In five years, he calculated, he would double the numbers. He saw the coming importance of the modern side, and especially of science. Personally, he detested "stinks," but he knew what an effect he would produce with a great laboratory fitted with the very best appliances and directed by a highly qualified master. Then, again, an elaborate gymnasium must be built; there must be an engineer's shop, too, and a carpenter's as well. And people were beginning to complain that a Public School Education was of no use in the City. There must be a business master, an expert from the Stock Exchange who would see that this reproach was removed. Then he considered that a large number of the boys belonged to the land-owning class. Why should a country gentleman be at the mercy of his agent, forced for lack of technical knowledge to accept statements which he could not check? It was clear that the management of land and great estates must have its part in the scheme; and, again, the best-known of the Crammers must be bought on his own terms, so that the boys who wished to get into the Army or the Civil Service would be practically compelled to come to Lupton. Already he saw paragraphs in the *Guardian* and *The Times* - in all the papers - paragraphs which mentioned the fact that ninety-five per cent of the successful candidates for the Indian Civil Service had received their education at the foundation of "stout old Martin Rolle." Meanwhile, in all this flood of novelty, the old traditions should be maintained with more vigour than ever. The classics should be taught as they never had been taught. Every one of the masters on this side should be in the highest honours and, if possible, he would get famous men for the work - they should not merely be good, but also notorious scholars. Gee, the famous explorer in Crete, who had made an enormous mark in regions widely removed from the scholastic world by his wonderful book, *Dædalus*; or, *The Secret of the Labyrinth*, must come to Lupton at any price; and Maynard, who had discovered some most important Greek manuscripts in Egypt, he must have a form, too. Then there was Rendell, who had done so well with his *Thucydides*, and Davies, author of *The Olive of Athene*, a daring but most brilliant book which promised to upset the whole established theory of mythology - he would have such a staff as no school had ever dreamed of. "We shall have no difficulty about paying them," thought Horbury; "our numbers will go up by leaps and bounds, and the fees shall be five hundred pounds a year - and such terms will do us more good than anything."

He went into minute detail. He must take expert advice as to the advisability of the school farming on its own account, and so supplying the boys with meat, milk, bread, butter and vegetables at first cost. He believed it could be done; he would get a Scotch farmer from the Lowlands and make him superintendent at a handsome salary and with a share in the profits. There would be the splendid advertisement of "the whole dietary of the school supplied from the School Farms, under the supervision of Mr. David Anderson, formerly of Haddanneuk, the largest tenancy in the Duke of Ayr's estates." The food would be better and cheaper, too; but there would be no luxury. The "Spartan" card was always worth playing; one must strike the note of plain living in a luxurious age; there must be no losing of the old Public School severity. On the other hand, the boy's hands should be free to go into their own pockets; there should be no restraint here. If a boy chose to bring in *Dindonneau aux truffes* or *Pieds de mouton à la Ste Menehould* to help out his tea, that was his look-out. Why should not the school grant a concession to some big London firm, who would pay handsomely for the privilege of supplying the hungry lads with every kind of expensive dainty? The sum could be justly made a large one, as any competing shop could be promptly put out of bounds with reason or without it. On one side, *confiserie*; at the other counter, *charcuterie*; enormous prices could be charged to the wealthy boys of whom the school would be composed. Yet, on the other hand, the distinguished visitor - judge, bishop, peer or what not - would lunch at the Headmaster's house and eat the boys' dinner and go away saying it was quite the plainest and very many times the best meal he had ever tasted. There would be well-hung saddle of mutton, roasted and not baked; floury potatoes and cauliflower; apple pudding with real English cheese, with an excellent glass of the school beer, an honest and delicious beverage made of malt and hops in the well-found school brewery. Horbury knew enough of modern eating and drinking to understand that such a meal would be a choice rarity to nine rich people out of ten; and yet it was "Spartan," utterly devoid of luxury and ostentation.

Again, he passed from detail and minutiæ into great Napoleonic regions. A thousand boys at £500 a year; that would be an income for the school of five hundred thousand pounds! The profits would be gigantic, immense. After paying large, even extravagant, prices to the staff, after all building expenses had been deducted, he hardly dared to think how vast a sum would accrue year by year to the Trustees. The vision began to assume such magnificence that it became oppressive; it put on the splendours and delights of the hashish dream, which are too great and too piercing for mortal hearts to bear. And yet it was no mirage; there was not a step that could not be demonstrated, shown to be based on hard; matter-of-fact business considerations. He tried to keep back his growing excitement, to argue with himself that he was dealing in visions, but the facts were too obstinate. He saw that it would be his part to work the same miracle in the scholastic world as the great American storekeepers had operated in the world of retail trade. The principle was precisely the same: instead of a hundred small shops making comparatively modest and humdrum profits you had the vast emporium doing business on the gigantic scale with vastly diminished expenses and vastly increased rewards.

Here again was a hint. He had thought of America, and he knew that here was an inexhaustible gold mine, that no other scholastic prospector had even dreamed of. The rich American was notoriously hungry for everything that was English, from frock-coats to pedigrees. He had never thought of sending his son to an English Public School because he considered the system hopelessly behind the times. But the new translated Lupton would be to other Public Schools as a New York hotel of the latest fashion is to a village beer-shop. And yet the young millionaire would grow up in the company of the sons of the English gentlemen, imbibing the unique culture of English life, while at the same time he enjoyed all the advantages of modern ideas, modern science and modern business training. Land was still comparatively cheap at Lupton; the school must buy it quietly, indirectly, by degrees, and then pile after pile of vast buildings rose before his eyes. He saw the sons of the rich drawn from all the ends of the world to the Great School, there to learn the secret of the Anglo-Saxons.

Chesson was mistaken in that idea of his, which he thought daring and original, of establishing a distinct Jewish House where the food should be "Kosher." The rich Jew who desired to send his son to an English Public School was, in nine cases out of ten, anxious to do so precisely because he wanted to sink his son's connection with Jewry in oblivion. He had heard Chesson talk of "our Christian duty to the seed of Israel" in this connection. The man was clearly a fool. No, the more Jews the better, but no Jewish House. And no Puseyism either: broad, earnest religious teaching, with a leaning to moderate Anglicanism, should be the faith of Lupton. As to this Chesson was, certainly, sound enough. He had always made a firm stand against ecclesiasticism in any form. Horbury knew the average English parent of the wealthier classes thoroughly; he knew that, though he generally called himself a Churchman, he was quite content to have his sons prepared for confirmation by a confessed Agnostic. Certainly this liberty must not be narrowed when Lupton became cosmopolitan. "We will retain all the dignified associations which belong to the Established Church," he said to himself, "and at the same time we shall be utterly free from the taint of over-emphasising dogmatic teaching." He had a sudden brilliant idea. Everybody in Church circles was saying that the English bishops were terribly overworked, that it was impossible for the most strenuous men with the best intentions to supervise effectually the huge dioceses that had descended from the sparsely populated England of the Middle Ages. Everywhere there was a demand for suffragans and more suffragans. In the last week's *Guardian* there were three letters on the subject, one from a clergyman in their own diocese. The Bishop had been attacked by some rabid ritualistic person, who had pointed out that nine out of every ten parishes had not so much as seen the colour of his hood ever since his appointment ten years before. The Archdeacon of Melby had replied in a capital letter, scathing and yet humorous. Horbury turned to the paper on the table beside his chair and looked up the letter. "In the first place," wrote the Archdeacon, "your correspondent does not seem to have realised that the *ethoes* of the Diocese of Melby is not identical with that of sacerdotalism. The sturdy folk of the Midlands have not yet, I am thankful to say, forgotten the lessons of our great Reformation. They have no wish to see a revival of the purely mechanical religion of the Middle Ages - of the system of a sacrificing priesthood and of sacraments efficacious *ex opere operato*. Hence they do not regard the episcopate quite in the same light as your correspondent 'Senex,' who, it seems to me, looks upon a bishop as a sort of Christianised 'medicine-man,' endowed with certain mysterious thaumaturgic powers which have descended to him by an (imaginary) spiritual succession. This was not the view of Hooker, nor, I venture to say, has it ever been the view of the really representative divines of the Established Church of England.

"Still," the Archdeacon went on, "it must be admitted that the present diocese of Melby is unwieldy and, it may be fairly said, unworkable."

Then there followed the humorous anecdote of Sir Boyle Roche and the Bird, and finally the Archdeacon emitted the prayer that God in His own good time would put it into the hearts of our rulers in Church and State to give their good Bishop an episcopal curate.

Horbury got up from his chair and paced up and down the study; his excitement was so great that he could keep quiet no longer. His cigar had gone out long ago, and he had barely sipped the whisky and soda. His eyes glittered with excitement. Circumstances seemed positively to be playing into his hands; the dice of the world were being loaded in his favour. He was like Bel Ami at his wedding. He almost began to believe in Providence.

For he was sure it could be managed. Here was a general feeling that no one man could do the work of the diocese. There must be a suffragan, and Lupton must give the new Bishop his title. No other town was possible. Dunham had certainly been a see in the eighth century, but it was now little more than a village and a village served by a miserable little branch line; whereas Lupton was on the great main track of the Midland system, with easy connections to every part of the country. The Archdeacon, who was also a peer, would undoubtedly become the first Bishop of Lupton, and he should be the titular chaplain of the Great School! "Chaplain! The Right Reverend Lord Selwyn, Lord Bishop of Lupton." Horbury gasped; it was too magnificent, too splendid. He knew Lord Selwyn quite well and had no doubt as to his acceptance. He was a poor man, and there would be no difficulty whatever in establishing a *modus*. The Archdeacon was just the man for the place. He was no pedantic theologian, but a broad, liberal-minded man of the world. Horbury remembered, almost with ecstasy, that he had lectured all over the United States with immense success. The American Press had been enthusiastic, and the First Congregational Church of Chicago had implored Selwyn to accept its call, preach what he liked and pocket an honorarium of twenty-five thousand dollars a year. And, on the other hand, what could the most orthodox desire safer than a chaplain who was not only a bishop, but a peer of the realm? Wonderful! Here were the three birds - Liberalism, Orthodoxy and Reverence for the House of Lords - caught safe and secure in this one net.

The games? They should be maintained in all their glory, rather on an infinitely more splendid scale. Cricket and sticker (the Lupton hockey), rackets and fives, should be all encouraged; and more, Lupton should be the only school to possess a tennis court. The noble *jeu de paume*, the game of kings, the most aristocratic of all sports, should have a worthy home at Lupton. They would train champions; they would have both French and English markers skilled in the latest developments of the *chemin de fer* service. "Better than half a yard, I think," said Horbury to himself; "they will have to do their best to beat that."

But he placed most reliance on rocker. This was the Lupton football, a variant as distinctive in its way as the Eton Wall Game. People have thought that the name is a sort of portmanteau word, a combination of Rugger and Soccer; but in reality the title was derived from the field where the game used to be played in old days by the townsfolk. As in many other places, football at Lupton had been originally an excuse for a faction-fight between two parishes in the town - St. Michael's and St. Paul's-in-the-Fields. Every year, on Shrove Tuesday, the townsfolk, young and old, had proceeded to the Town Field and had fought out their differences with considerable violence. The field was broken land: a deep, sluggish stream crossed one angle of it, and in the middle there were quarries and jagged limestone rocks. Hence football was called in the town "playing rocks," for, indeed, it was considered an excellent point of play to hurl a man over the edge of the quarry on to the rocks beneath, and so late as 1830 a certain Jonas Simpson of St. Michael's had had his spine broken in this way. However, as a boy from St. Paul's was drowned in the Wand the same day, the game was always reckoned a draw. It was from the peculiarities of this old English sport that the school had constructed its game. The Town Field had, of course, long been stolen from the townsfolk and built over; but the boys had, curiously enough, perpetuated the tradition of its peculiarities in a kind of football ritual. For, besides the two goals, one part of the field was marked by a line of low white posts: these indicated the course of a non-existent Wand brook, and in the line of these posts it was lawful to catch an opponent by the throat and choke him till he turned black in the face - the best substitute for drowning that the revisers of the game could imagine. Again: about the centre of the field two taller posts indicated the position of the quarries, and between these you might be hit or kicked full in the stomach without the smallest ground of complaint: the stroke being a milder version of the old fall on the rocks.

There were many other like amenities in rocker; and Horbury maintained it was by far the manliest variant of the game. For this pleasing sport he now designed a world-wide fame. Rocker should be played wherever the English flag floated: east and west, north and south; from Hong Kong to British Columbia; in Canada and New Zealand there should be the *Temenoi* of this great rite; and the traveller seeing the mystic enclosure - the two goals, the line of little posts marking "brooks" and the two poles indicating "quarries" - should know English soil as surely as by the Union Jack. The technical terms of rocker should become a part of the great Anglo-Saxon inheritance; the whole world should hear of "bully-downs" and "tokering," of "outsides" and "rammers." It would require working, but it was to be done: articles in the magazines and in the Press; perhaps a story of school life, a new *Tom Brown* must be written. The Midlands and the North must be shown that there was money in it, and the rest would be easy.

One thing troubled Horbury. His mind was full of the new and splendid buildings that were to be erected, but he was aware that antiquity still counted for something, and unfortunately Lupton could show very little that was really antique. Forty years before, Stanley, the first reforming Headmaster, had pulled down the old High School. There were prints of it: it was a half-timbered, fifteenth-century building, with a wavering roof-line and an overhanging upper story; there were dim, leaded windows and a grey arched porch - an ugly old barn, Stanley called it. Scott was called in and built the present High School, a splendid hall in red brick: French thirteenth-century, with Venetian detail; it was much admired. But Horbury was sorry that the old school had been destroyed; he saw for the first time that it might have been made a valuable attraction. Then again, Dowsing, who succeeded Stanley, had knocked the cloisters all to bits; there was only one side of the quadrangle left, and this had been boarded up and used as a gardeners' shed. Horbury did not know what to say of the destruction of the Cross that used to stand in the centre of the quad. No doubt Dowsing was right in thinking it superstitious; still, it might have been left as a curiosity and shown to visitors, just as the instruments of bygone cruelty - the rack and the Iron Maid - are preserved and exhibited to wondering sightseers. There was no real danger of any superstitious adoration of the Cross; it was, as a matter of fact, as harmless as the axe and block at the Tower of London; Dowsing had ruined what might have been an important asset in the exploitation of the school.

Still, perhaps the loss was not altogether irreparable. High School was gone and could not be recovered; but the cloisters might be restored and the Cross, too. Horbury knew that the monument in front of Charing Cross Railway Station was considered by many to be a genuine antique: why not get a good man to build them a Cross? Not like the old one, of course; that "Fair Roode with our Deare Ladie Saint Marie and Saint John," and, below, the stories of the blissful Saints and Angels - that would never do. But a vague, Gothic erection, with plenty of kings and queens, imaginary benefactors of the school, and a small cast-iron cross at the top: that could give no offence to anybody, and might pass with nine people out of ten as a genuine remnant of the Middle Ages. It could be made of soft stone and allowed to weather for a few years; then a coat of invisible anti-corrosive fluid would preserve carvings and imagery that would already appear venerable in decay. There was no need to make any precise statements: parents and the public might be allowed to draw their own conclusions.

Horbury was neglecting nothing. He was building up a great scheme in his mind, and to him it seemed that every detail was worth attending to, while at the same time he did not lose sight of the whole effect. He believed in finish: there must be no rough edges. It seemed to him that a school legend must be invented. The real history was not quite what he wanted, though it might work in with a more decorative account of Lupton's origins. One might use the *Textus Receptus* of Martin Rolle's Foundation - the bequest of land c. 1430 to build and maintain a school where a hundred boys should be taught grammar, and ten poor scholars and six priests should pray for the Founder's soul. This was well enough, but one might hint that Martin Rolle really refounded and re-endowed a school of Saxon origin, probably established by King Alfred himself in Luppa's Tun. Then, again, who could show that Shakespeare had not visited Lupton? His famous schoolboy, "creeping like snail unwillingly to school," might very possibly have been observed by the poet as he strolled by the banks of the Wand. Many famous men might have received their education at Lupton; it would not be difficult to make a plausible list of such. It must be done carefully and cautiously, with such phrases as "it has always been a tradition at Lupton that Sir Walter Raleigh received part of his education at the school"; or, again, "an earlier generation of Luptonians remembered the initials 'W. S. S. on A.' cut deeply in the mantel of old High School, now, unfortunately, demolished." Antiquarians would laugh? Possibly; but who cared about antiquarians? For the average man "Charing" was derived from "*chère reine*," and he loved to have it so, and Horbury intended to appeal to the average man. Though he was a schoolmaster he was no recluse, and he had marked the ways of the world from his quiet study in Lupton; hence he understood the immense value of a grain of quackery in all schemes which are meant to appeal to mortals. It was a deadly mistake to suppose that anything which was all quackery would be a success - a permanent success, at all events; it was a deadlier mistake still to suppose that anything quite devoid of quackery could pay handsomely. The average English palate would shudder at the flavour of *aioli*, but it would be charmed by the insertion of that *petit point d'ail* which turned mere goodness into triumph and laurelled perfection. And there was no need to mention the word "garlic" before the guests. Lupton was not going to be all garlic: it was to be infinitely the best scholastic dish that had ever been served - the ingredients should be unsurpassed and unsurpassable. But - King Alfred's foundation of a school at Luppa's Tun, and that "W. S. S. on A." cut deeply on the mantel of the vanished High School - these and legends like unto them, these would be the last touch, *le petit point d'ail*.

It was a great scheme, wonderful and glorious; and the most amazing thing about it was that it was certain to be realised. There was not a flaw from start to finish. The Trustees were certain to appoint him - he had that from a sure quarter - and it was but a question of a year or two, perhaps only of a month or two, before all this great and golden vision should be converted into hard and tangible fact. He drank off his glass of whisky and soda; it had become flat and brackish, but to him it was nectar, since it was flavoured with ecstasy.

He frowned suddenly as he went upstairs to his room. An unpleasant recollection had intruded for a moment on his amazing fantasy; but he dismissed the thought as soon as it arose. That was all over, there could be no possibility of trouble from that direction; and so, his mind filled with images, he fell asleep and saw Lupton as the centre of the whole world, like Jerusalem in the ancient maps.

A student of the deep things of mysticism has detected a curious element of comedy in the management of human concerns; and there certainly seems a touch of humour in the fact that on this very night, while Horbury was building the splendid Lupton of the future, the palace of his thought and his life was shattered for ever into bitter dust and nothingness. But so it was. The Dread Arrest had been solemnly recognised, and that wretched canonry at Wareham was irrevocably pronounced for doom. Fantastic were the elements of forces that had gone to the ordering of this great sentence: raw corn spirit in the guise of sherry, the impertinence (or what seemed such) of an elderly clergyman, a boiled leg of mutton, a troublesome and disobedient boy, and - another person.

CHAPTER II

I

He was standing in a wild, bare country. Something about it seemed vaguely familiar: the land rose and fell in dull and weary undulations, in a vast circle of dun ploughland and grey meadow, bounded by a dim horizon without promise or hope, dreary as a prison wall. The infinite melancholy of an autumn evening brooded heavily over all the world, and the sky was hidden by livid clouds.

It all brought back to him some far-off memory, and yet he knew that he gazed on that sad plain for the first time. There was a deep and heavy silence over all; a silence unbroken by so much as the fluttering of a leaf. The trees seemed of a strange shape, and strange were the stunted thorns dotted about the broken field in which he stood. A little path at his feet, bordered by the thorn bushes, wandered away to the left into the dim twilight; it had about it some indefinable air of mystery, as if it must lead one down into a mystic region where all earthly things are forgotten and lost for ever.

He sat down beneath the bare, twisted boughs of a great tree and watched the dreary land grow darker and yet darker; he wondered, half-consciously, where he was and how he had come to that place, remembering, faintly, tales of like adventure. A man passed by a familiar wall one day, and opening a door before unnoticed, found himself in a new world of unsurmised and marvellous experiences. Another man shot an arrow farther than any of his friends and became the husband of the fairy. Yet - this was not fairyland; these were rather the sad fields and unhappy graves of the underworld than the abode of endless pleasures and undying delights. And yet in all that he saw there was the promise of great wonder.

Only one thing was clear to him. He knew that he was Ambrose, that he had been driven from great and unspeakable joys into miserable exile and banishment. He had come from a far, far place by a hidden way, and darkness had closed about him, and bitter drink and deadly meat were given him, and all gladness was hidden from him. This was all he could remember; and now he was astray, he knew not how or why, in this wild, sad land, and the night descended dark upon him.

Suddenly there was, as it were, a cry far away in the shadowy silence, and the thorn bushes began to rustle before a shrilling wind that rose as the night came down. At this summons the heavy clouds broke up and dispersed, fleeting across the sky, and the pure heaven appeared with the last rose flush of the sunset dying from it, and there shone the silver light of the evening star. Ambrose's heart was drawn up to this light as he gazed: he saw that the star grew greater and greater; it advanced towards him through the air; its beams pierced to his soul as if they were the sound of a silver trumpet. An ocean of white splendour flowed over him: he dwelt within the star.

It was but for a moment; he was still sitting beneath the tree of the twisted branches. But the sky was now clear and filled with a great peace; the wind had fallen and a more happy light shone on the great plain. Ambrose was thirsty, and then he saw that beside the tree there was a well, half hidden by the arching roots that rose above it. The water was still and shining, as though it were a mirror of black marble, and marking the brim was a great stone on which were cut the letters:

"FONS VITAE IMMORTALIS."

He rose and, bending over the well, put down his lips to drink, and his soul and body were filled as with a flood of joy. Now he knew that all his days of exile he had borne with pain and grief a heavy, weary body. There had been dolours in every limb and achings in every bone; his feet had dragged upon the ground, slowly, wearily, as the feet of those who go in chains. But dim, broken spectres, miserable shapes and crooked images of the world had his eyes seen; for they were eyes bleared with sickness, darkened by the approach of death. Now, indeed, he clearly beheld the shining vision of things immortal. He drank great draughts of the dark, glittering water, drinking, it seemed, the light of the reflected stars; and he was filled with life. Every sinew, every muscle, every particle of the deadly flesh shuddered and quickened in the communion of that well-water. The nerves and veins rejoiced together; all his being leapt with gladness, and as one finger touched another, as he still bent over the well, a spasm of exquisite pleasure quivered and thrilled through his body. His heart throbbed with bliss that was unendurable; sense and intellect and soul and spirit were, as it were, sublimed into one white flame of delight. And all the while it was known to him that these were but the least of the least of the pleasures of the kingdom, but the overrunnings and base tricklings of the great supernal cup. He saw, without amazement, that, though the sun had set, the sky now began to flush and redden as if with the northern light. It was no longer the evening, no longer the time of the procession of the dusky night. The darkness doubtless had passed away in mortal hours while for an infinite moment he tasted immortal drink; and perhaps one drop of that water was endless life. But now it was the preparation for the day. He heard the words:

Dies venit, dies
Tua In qua reflorent omnia.

They were uttered within his heart, and he saw that all was being made ready for a great festival. Over everything there was a hush of expectation; and as he gazed he knew that he was no longer in that weary land of dun ploughland and grey meadow, of the wild, bare trees and strange stunted thorn bushes. He was on a hillside, lying on the verge of a great wood; beneath, in the valley, a brook sang faintly under the leaves of the silvery willows; and beyond, far in the east, a vast wall of rounded mountain rose serene towards the sky. All about him was the green world of the leaves: odours of the summer night, deep in the mystic heart of the wood, odours of many flowers, and the cool breath rising from the singing stream mingled in his nostrils. The world whitened to the dawn, and then, as the light grew clear, the rose clouds blossomed in the sky and, answering, the earth seemed to glitter with rose-red sparks and glints of flame. All the east became as a garden of roses, red flowers of living light shone over the mountain, and as the beams of the sun lit up the circle of the earth a bird's song began from a tree within the wood. Then were heard the modulations of a final and exultant ecstasy, the chant of liberation, a magistral In Exitu; there was the melody of rejoicing trills, of unwearied, glad reiterations of choirs ever aspiring, prophesying the coming of the great feast, singing the eternal antiphon.

As the song aspired into the heights, so there aspired suddenly before him the walls and pinnacles of a great church set upon a high hill. It was far off, and yet as though it were close at hand he saw all the delicate and wonderful imagery cut in its stones. The great door in the west was a miracle: every flower and leaf, every reed and fern, were clustered in the work of the capitals, and in the round arch above moulding within moulding showed all the beasts that God has made. He saw the rose-window, a maze of fretted tracery, the high lancets of the fair hall, the marvellous buttresses, set like angels about this holy house, whose pinnacles were as a place of many springing trees. And high above the vast, far-lifted vault of the roof rose up the spire, golden in the light. The bells were ringing for the feast; he heard from within the walls the roll and swell and triumph of the organ:

O pius o bonus o placidus sonus hymnus eorum.

He knew not how he had taken his place in this great procession, how, surrounded by ministrants in white, he too bore his part in endless litanies. He knew not through what strange land they passed in their fervent, admirable order, following their banners and their symbols that glanced on high before them. But that land stood ever, it seemed, in a clear, still air, crowned with golden sunlight; and so there were those who bore great torches of wax, strangely and beautifully adorned with golden and vermilion ornaments. The delicate flame of these tapers burned steadily in the still sunlight, and the glittering silver censers as they rose and fell tossed a pale cloud into the air. They delayed, now and again, by wayside shrines, giving thanks for unutterable compassions, and, advancing anew, the blessed company surged onward, moving to its unknown goal in the far blue mountains that rose beyond the plain. There were faces and shapes of awful beauty about him; he saw those in whose eyes were the undying lamps of heaven, about whose heads the golden hair was as an aureole; and there were they that above the girded vesture of white wore dyed garments, and as they advanced around their feet there was the likeness of dim flames.

The great white array had vanished and he was alone. He was tracking a secret path that wound in and out through the thickets of a great forest. By solitary pools of still water, by great oaks, worlds of green leaves, by fountains and streams of water, by the bubbling, mossy sources of the brooks he followed this hidden way, now climbing and now descending, but still mounting upward, still passing, as he knew, farther and farther from all the habitations of men. Through the green boughs now he saw the shining sea-water; he saw the land of the old saints, all the divisions of the land that men had given to them for God; he saw their churches, and it seemed as if he could hear, very faintly, the noise of the ringing of their holy bells. Then, at last, when he had crossed the Old Road, and had gone by the Lightning-struck Land and the Fisherman's Well, he found, between the forest and the mountain, a very ancient and little chapel; and now he heard the bell of the saint ringing clearly and so sweetly that it was as it were the singing of the angels. Within it was very dark and there was silence. He knelt and saw scarcely that the chapel was divided into two parts by a screen that rose up to the round roof. There was a glinting of shapes as if golden figures were painted on this screen, and through the joinings of its beams there streamed out thin needles of white splendour as if within there was a light greater than that of the sun at noonday. And the flesh began to tremble, for all the place was filled with the odours of Paradise, and he heard the ringing of the Holy Bell and the voices of the choir that out-sang the Fairy Birds of Rhiannon, crying and proclaiming:

> *Glory and praise to the Conqueror of Death:*
> *to the Fountain of Life Unending.*

Nine times they sang this anthem, and then the whole place was filled with blinding light. For a door in the screen had been opened, and there came forth an old man, all in shining white, on whose head was a gold crown. Before him went one who rang the bell; on each side there were young men with torches; and in his hands he bore the *Mystery of Mysteries* wrapped about in veils of gold and of all colours, so that it might not be discerned; and so he passed before the screen, and the light of heaven burst forth from that which he held. Then he entered in again by a door that was on the other side, and the Holy Things were hidden.

And Ambrose heard from within an awful voice and the words:

> *Woe and great sorrow are on him, for he hath looked unworthily into*
> *the Tremendous Mysteries, and on the Secret Glory which is hidden*
> *from the Holy Angels.*

II

"Poetry is the only possible way of saying anything that is worth saying at all." This was an axiom that, in later years, Ambrose Meyrick's friends were forced to hear at frequent intervals. He would go on to say that he used the term poetry in its most liberal sense, including in it all mystic or symbolic prose, all painting and statuary that was worthy to be called art, all great architecture, and all true music. He meant, it is to be presumed, that the mysteries can only be conveyed by symbols; unfortunately, however, he did not always make it quite clear that this was the proposition that he intended to utter, and thus offence was sometimes given - as, for example, to the scientific gentleman who had been brought to Meyrick's rooms and went away early, wondering audibly and sarcastically whether "your clever friend" wanted to metrify biology and set Euclid to Bach's Organ Fugues.

However, the Great Axiom (as he called it) was the justification that he put forward in defence of the notes on which the previous section is based.

"Of course," he would say, "the symbolism is inadequate; but that is the defect of speech of any kind when you have once ventured beyond the multiplication table and the jargon of the Stock Exchange. Inadequacy of expression is merely a minor part of the great tragedy of humanity. Only an ass thinks that he has succeeded in uttering the perfect content of his thought without either excess or defect."

"Then, again," he might go on, "the symbolism would very likely be misleading to a great many people; but what is one to do? I believe many good people find Turner mad and Dickens tiresome. And if the great sometimes fail, what hope is there for the little? We cannot all be - well - popular novelists of the day."

Of course, the notes in question were made many years after the event they commemorate; they were the man's translation of all the wonderful and inexpressible emotions of the boy; and, as Meyrick puts it, many "words" (or symbols) are used in them which were unknown to the lad of fifteen.

"Nevertheless," he said, "they are the best words that I can find."

As has been said, the Old Grange was a large, roomy house; a space could easily have been found for half a dozen more boys if the High Usher had cared to be bothered with them. As it was, it was a favour to be at Horbury's, and there was usually some personal reason for admission. Pelly, for example, was the son of an old friend; Bates was a distant cousin; and Rawson's father was the master of a small Grammar School in the north with which certain ancestral Horburys were somehow connected. The Old Grange was a fine large Caroline house; it had a grave front of red brick, mellowed with age, tier upon tier of tall, narrow windows, flush with the walls, and a high-pitched, red-tiled roof. Above the front door was a rich and curious wooden pent-house, deeply carven; and within there was plenty of excellent panelling, and some good mantelpieces, added, it would seem, somewhere about the Adam period. Horbury had seen its solid and comfortable merits and had bought the freehold years before at a great bargain. The school was increasing rapidly even in those days, and he knew that before long more houses would be required. If he left Lupton he would be able to let the Old Grange easily - he might almost put it up for auction - and the rent would represent a return of fifty per cent on his investment. Many of the rooms were large; of a size out of all proportion to the boys' needs, and at a very trifling expense partitions might be made and the nine or ten available rooms be subdivided into studies for twenty or even twenty-five boys. Nature had gifted the High Usher with a careful, provident mind in all things, both great and small; and it is but fair to add that on his leaving Lupton for Wareham he found his anticipations more than justified. To this day Charles Horbury, his nephew, a high Government official, draws a comfortable income from his uncle's most prudent investment, and the house easily holds its twenty-five boys. Rainy, who took the place from Horbury, was an ingenious fellow and hit upon a capital plan for avoiding the expense of making new windows for some of the subdivided studies. After thoughtful consideration he caused the wooden partitions which were put up to stop short of the ceiling by four inches, and by this device the study with a window lighted the study that had none; and, as Rainy explained to some of the parents, a diffused light was really better for the eyes than a direct one.

In the old days, when Ambrose Meyrick was being made a man of, the four boys "rattled," as it were, in the big house. They were scattered about in odd corners, remote from each other, and it seemed from everybody else. Meyrick's room was the most isolated of any, but it was also the most comfortable in winter, since it was over the kitchen, to the extreme left of the house. This part, which was hidden from the road by the boughs of a great cedar, was an after-thought, a Georgian addition in grey brick, and rose only to two stories, and in the one furnished room out of the three or four over the kitchen and offices slept Ambrose. He wished his days could be as quiet and retired as his nights. He loved the shadows that were about his bed even on the brightest mornings in summer; for the cedar boughs were dense, and ivy had been allowed to creep about the panes of the window; so the light entered dim and green, filtered through the dark boughs and the ivy tendrils.

Here, then, after the hour of ten each night, he dwelt secure. Now and again Mr. Horbury would pay nocturnal surprise visits to see that all lights were out; but, happily, the stairs at the end of the passage, being old and badly fitted, gave out a succession of cracks like pistol shots if the softest foot was set on them. It was simple, therefore, on hearing the first of these reports, to extinguish the candle in the small secret lantern (held warily so that no gleam of light should appear from under the door) and to conceal the lantern under the bed-clothes.

One wetted one's finger and pinched at the flame, so there was no smell of the expiring snuff, and the lantern slide was carefully drawn to guard against the possibility of suspicious grease-marks on the linen. It was perfect; and old Horbury's visits, which were rare enough, had no terrors for Ambrose.

So that night, while the venom of the cane still rankled in his body, though it had ceased to disturb his mind, instead of going to bed at once, according to the regulations, he sat for a while on his box seeking a clue in a maze of odd fancies and conceits. He took off his clothes and wrapped his aching body in the rug from the bed, and presently, blowing out the official paraffin lamp, he lit his candle, ready at the first warning creak on the stairs to douse the glim and leap between the sheets.

Odd enough were his first cogitations. He was thinking how very sorry he was to have hit Pelly that savage blow and to have endangered Rawson's eyesight by the hard boards of the dictionary! This was eccentric, for he had endured from those two young Apaches every extremity of unpleasantness for upwards of a couple of years. Pelly was not by any means an evil lad: he was stupid and beefy within and without, and the great Public School system was transmuting him, in the proper course and by the proper steps, into one of those Brave Average Boobies whom Meyrick used to rail against afterwards. Pelly, in all probability (his fortunes have not been traced), went into the Army and led the milder and more serious subalterns the devil's own life. In India he "lay doggo" with great success against some hill tribe armed with seventeenth-century muskets and rather barbarous knives; he seems to have been present at that "Conference of the Powers" described so brightly by Mr. Kipling. Promoted to a captaincy, he fought with conspicuous bravery in South Africa, winning the Victoria Cross for his rescue of a wounded private at the instant risk of his own life, and he finally led his troop into a snare set by an old farmer; a rabbit of average intelligence would have smelt and evaded it.

For Rawson one is sorry, but one cannot, in conscience, say much that is good, though he has been praised for his tact. He became domestic chaplain to the Bishop of Dorchester, whose daughter Emily he married.

But in those old days there was very little to choose between them, from Meyrick's point of view. Each had displayed a quite devilish ingenuity in the art of annoyance, in the whole cycle of jeers and sneers and "scores," as known to the schoolboy, and they were just proceeding to more active measures. Meyrick had borne it all meekly; he had returned kindly and sometimes quaint answers to the unceasing stream of remarks that were meant to wound his feelings, to make him look a fool before any boys that happened to be about. He had only countered with a mild: "What do you do that for, Pelly?" when the brave one smacked his head. "Because I hate sneaks and funks," Pelly had replied and Meyrick said no more. Rawson took a smaller size in victims when it was a question of physical torments; but he had invented a most offensive tale about Meyrick and had told it all over the school, where it was universally believed. In a word, the two had done their utmost to reduce him to a state of utter misery; and now he was sorry that he had punched the nose of one and bombarded the other with a dictionary!

The fact was that his forebearance had not been all cowardice; it is, indeed, doubtful whether he was in the real sense a coward at all. He went in fear, it is true, all his days, but what he feared was not the insult, but the intention, the malignancy of which the insult, or the blow, was the outward sign. The fear of a mad bull is quite distinct from the horror with which most people look upon a viper; it was the latter feeling which made Meyrick's life a burden to him. And again there was a more curious shade of feeling; and that was the intense hatred that he felt to the mere thought of "scoring" off an antagonist, of beating down the enemy. He was a much sharper lad than either Rawson or Pelly; he could have retorted again and again with crushing effect, but he held his tongue, for all such victories were detestable to him. And this odd sentiment governed all his actions and feelings; he disliked "going up" in form, he disliked winning a game, not through any acquired virtue, but by inherent nature. Poe would have understood Meyrick's feelings; but then the author of *The Imp of the Perverse* penetrated so deeply into the inmost secrets of humanity that Anglo-Saxon criticism has agreed in denouncing him as a wholly "inhuman" writer.

With Meyrick this mode of feeling had grown stronger by provocation; the more he was injured, the more he shrank from the thought of returning the injury. In a great measure the sentiment remained with him in later life. He would sally forth from his den in quest of fresh air on top of an omnibus and stroll peacefully back again rather than struggle for victory with the furious crowd. It was not so much that he disliked the physical contest: he was afraid of getting a seat! Quite naturally, he said that people who "pushed," in the metaphorical sense, always reminded him of the hungry little pigs fighting for the largest share of the wash; but he seemed to think that, whereas this course of action was natural in the little pigs, it was profoundly unnatural in the little men. But in his early boyhood he had carried this secret doctrine of his to its utmost limits; he had assumed, as it were, the rôle of the coward and the funk; he had, without any conscious religious motive certainly, but in obedience to an inward command, endeavoured to play the part of a Primitive Christian, of a religious, in a great Public School! *Ama nesciri et pro nihilo æstimari.* The maxim was certainly in his heart, though he had never heard it; but perhaps if he had searched the whole world over he could not have found a more impossible field for its exercise than this seminary, where the broad, liberal principles of Christianity were taught in a way that satisfied the Press, the public and the parents.

And he sat in his room and grieved over the fashion in which he had broken this discipline. Still, something had to be done: he was compelled to stay in this place, and he did not wish to be reduced to the imbecility of wretched little Phipps who had become at last more like a whimpering kitten with the mange than a human being. One had not the right to allow oneself to be made an idiot, so the principle had to be infringed - but externally only, never internally! Of that he was firmly resolved; and he felt secure in his recollection that there had been no anger in his heart. He resented the presence of Pelly and Rawson, certainly, but in the manner with which some people resent the presence of a cat, a mouse, or a black-beetle, as disagreeable objects which can't help being disagreeable objects. But his bashing of Pelly and his smashing of Rawson, his remarks (gathered from careful observation by the banks of the Lupton and Birmingham Canal); all this had been but the means to an end, the securing of peace and quiet for the future. He would not be murdered by this infernal Public School system either, after the fashion of Phipps - which was melancholy, or after the fashion of the rest - which was more melancholy still, since it is easier to recover from nervous breakdown than from suffusion of cant through the entire system, mental and spiritual. Utterly from his heart he abjured and renounced all the horrible shibboleths of the school, its sham enthusiasm, its "ethos," its "tone," its "loyal co-operation - masters and boys working together for the good of the whole school" - all its ridiculous fetish conventions and absurd observances, the joint contrivances of young fools and old knaves. But his resistance should be secret and not open, for a while; there should be no more "bashing" than was absolutely necessary.

And one thing he resolved upon - he would make all he could out of the place; he would work like a tiger and get all the Latin and Greek and French obtainable, in spite of the teaching and its imbecile pedantry. The school work must be done, so that trouble might be avoided, but here at night in his room he would really learn the languages they pottered over in form, wasting half their time in writing sham Ciceronian prose which would have made Cicero sick, and verse evil enough to cause Virgil to vomit. Then there was French, taught chiefly out of pompous eighteenth-century fooleries, with lists of irregular verbs to learn and Babylonish nonsense about the past participle, and many other rotten formulas and rules, giving to the whole tongue the air of a tiresome puzzle which had been dug up out of a prehistoric grave. This was not the French that he wanted; still, he could write out irregular verbs by day and learn the language at night. He wondered whether unhappy French boys had to learn English out of the *Rambler*, Blair's *Sermons* and Young's *Night Thoughts*. For he had some sort of smattering of English literature which a Public School boy has no business to possess. So he went on with this mental tirade of his: one is not over-wise at fifteen. It is true enough, perhaps, that the French of the average English schoolboy is something fit to move only pity and terror; it may be true also that nobody except Deans and schoolmasters seems to bring away even the formulas and sacred teachings (such as the Optative mystery and the Doctrine of Dum) of the two great literatures. There is, doubtless, a good deal to be said on the subject of the Public Schoolman's knowledge of the history and literature of his own country; an infinite deal of comic stuff might be got out of his views and acquirements in the great science of theology - still let us say, *Floreat*!

Meyrick turned from his review of the wisdom of his elders and instructors to more intimate concerns. There were a few cuts of that vigorous cane which still stung and hurt most abominably, for skill or fortune had guided Mr. Horbury's hand so that he had been enabled here and there to get home twice in the same place, and there was one particular weal on the left arm where the flesh, purple and discoloured, had swelled up and seemed on the point of bursting. It was no longer with rage, but with a kind of rapture, that he felt the pain and smarting; he looked upon the ugly marks of the High Usher's evil humours as though they had been a robe of splendour. For he knew nothing of that bad sherry, nothing of the Head's conversation; he knew that when Pelly had come in quite as late it had only been a question of a hundred lines, and so he persisted in regarding himself as a martyr in the cause of those famous "Norman arches," which was the cause of that dear dead enthusiast, his father, who loved Gothic architecture and all other beautiful "unpractical" things with an undying passion. As soon as Ambrose could walk he had begun his pilgrimages to hidden mystic shrines; his father had led him over the wild lands to places known perhaps only to himself, and there, by the ruined stones, by the smooth hillock, had told the tale of the old vanished time, the time of the "old saints."

III

It was for this blessed and wonderful learning, he said to himself, that he had been beaten, that his body had been scored with red and purple stripes. He remembered his father's oft-repeated exclamation, "cythrawl Sais!" He understood that the phrase damned not Englishmen qua Englishmen, but Anglo-Saxonism - the power of the creed that builds Manchester, that "does business," that invents popular dissent, representative government, adulteration, suburbs, and the Public School system. It was, according to his father, the creed of "the Prince of this world," the creed that made for comfort, success, a good balance at the bank, the praise of men, the sensible and tangible victory and achievement; and he bade his little boy, who heard everything and understood next to nothing, fly from it, hate it and fight against it as he would fight against the devil - "and," he would add, "it *is* the only devil you are ever likely to come across."

And the little Ambrose had understood not much of all this, and if he had been asked - even at fifteen - what it all meant, he would probably have said that it was a great issue between Norman mouldings and Mr. Horbury, an Armageddon of

Selden Abbey *versus* rocker. Indeed, it is doubtful whether old Nicholas Meyrick would have been very much clearer, for he forgot everything that might be said on the other side. He forgot that Anglo-Saxonism (save in the United States of America) makes generally for equal laws; that civil riot ("Labour" movements, of course, excepted) is more a Celtic than a Saxon vice; that the penalty of burning alive is unknown amongst Anglo-Saxons, unless the provocation be extreme; that Englishmen have substituted "Indentured Labour" for the old-world horrors of slavery; that English justice smites the guilty rich equally with the guilty poor; that men are no longer poisoned with swift and secret drugs, though somewhat unwholesome food may still be sold very occasionally. Indeed, the old Meyrick once told his rector that he considered a brothel a house of sanctity compared with a modern factory, and he was beginning to relate some interesting tales concerning the Three Gracious Courtesans of the Isle of Britain when the rector fled in horror - he came from Sydenham. And all this was a nice preparation for Lupton.

A wonderful joy, an ecstasy of bliss, swelled in Ambrose's heart as he assured himself that he was a witness, though a mean one, for the old faith, for the faith of secret and beautiful and hidden mysteries as opposed to the faith of rocker and sticker and mucker, and "the thought of the school as an inspiring motive in life" - the text on which the Head had preached the Sunday before. He bared his arms and kissed the purple swollen flesh and prayed that it might ever be so, that in body and mind and spirit he might ever be beaten and reviled and made ridiculous for the sacred things, that he might ever be on the side of the despised and the unsuccessful, that his life might ever be in the shadow - in the shadow of the mysteries.

He thought of the place in which he was, of the hideous school, the hideous town, the weary waves of the dun Midland scenery bounded by the dim, hopeless horizon; and his soul revisited the faery hills and woods and valleys of the West. He remembered how, long ago, his father had roused him early from sleep in the hush and wonder of a summer morning. The whole world was still and windless; all the magic odours of the night rose from the earth, and as they crossed the lawn the silence was broken by the enchanted song of a bird rising from a thorn tree by the gate. A high white vapour veiled the sky, and they only knew that the sun had risen by the brightening of this veil, by the silvering of the woods and the meadows and the water in the rejoicing brook. They crossed the road, and crossed the brook in the field beneath, by the old foot-bridge tremulous with age, and began to climb the steep hillside that one could see from the windows, and, the ridge of the hill once surmounted, the little boy found himself in an unknown land: he looked into deep, silent valleys, watered by trickling streams; he saw still woods in that dreamlike morning air; he saw winding paths that climbed into yet remoter regions. His father led him onward till they came to a lonely height

- they had walked scarcely two miles, but to Ambrose it seemed a journey into another world - and showed him certain irregular markings in the turf.

And Nicholas Meyrick murmured:

> *The cell of Iltyd is by the seashore,*
> *The ninth wave washes its altar,*
> *There is a fair shrine in the land of Morgan.*
>
> *The cell of Dewi is in the City of the Legions,*
> *Nine altars owe obedience to it,*
> *Sovereign is the choir that sings about it.*
>
> *The cell of Cybi is the treasure of Gwent,*
> *Nine hills are its perpetual guardians,*
> *Nine songs befit the memory of the saint.*

"See," he said, "there are the Nine Hills." He pointed them out to the boy, telling him the tale of the saint and his holy bell, which they said had sailed across the sea from Syon and had entered the Severn, and had entered the Usk, and had entered the Soar, and had entered the Canthwr; and so one day the saint, as he walked beside the little brook that almost encompassed the hill in its winding course, saw the bell "that was made of metal that no man might comprehend," floating under the alders, and crying:

> *Sant, sant, sant,*
> *I sail from Syon*
> *To Cybi Sant!*

"And so sweet was the sound of that bell," Ambrose's father went on, "that they said it was as the joy of angels *ym Mharadwys*, and that it must have come not from the earthly, but from the heavenly and glorious Syon."

And there they stood in the white morning, on the uneven ground that marked the place where once the Saint rang to the sacrifice, where the quickening words were uttered after the order of the Old Mass of the Britons.

"And then came the Yellow Hag of Pestilence, that destroyed the bodies of the Cymri; then the Red Hag of Rome, that caused their souls to stray; last is come the Black Hag of Geneva, that sends body and soul quick to hell. No honour have the saints any more."

Then they turned home again, and all the way Ambrose thought he heard the bell as it sailed the great deeps from Syon, crying aloud: "Sant, Sant, Sant!" And the sound seemed to echo from the glassy water of the little brook, as it swirled and rippled over the shining stones circling round those lonely hills.

So they made strange pilgrimages over the beloved land, going farther and farther afield as the boy grew older. They visited deep wells in the heart of the woods, where a few broken stones, perhaps, were the last remains of the hermitage. "Ffynnon Ilar Bysgootwr - the well of Saint Ilar the Fisherman," Nicholas Meyrick would explain, and then would follow the story of Ilar; how no man knew whence he came or who his parents were. He was found, a little child, on a stone in a river in Armorica, by King Alan, and rescued by him. And ever after they discovered on the stone in the river where the child had lain every day a great and shining fish lying, and on this fish Ilar was nourished. And so he came with a great company of the saints to Britain, and wandered over all the land.

"So at last Ilar Sant came to this wood, which people now call St. Hilary's wood because they have forgotten all about Ilar. And he was weary with his wandering, and the day was very hot; so he stayed by this well and began to drink. And there on that great stone he saw the shining fish, and so he rested, and built an altar and a church of willow boughs, and offered the sacrifice not only for the quick and the dead, but for all the wild beasts of the woods and the streams.

"And when this blessed Ilar rang his holy bell and began to offer, there came not only the Prince and his servants, but all the creatures of the wood. There, under the hazel boughs, you might see the hare, which flies so swiftly from men, come gently and fall down, weeping greatly on account of the Passion of the Son of Mary. And, beside the hare, the weasel and the pole-cat would lament grievously in the manner of penitent sinners; and wolves and lambs together adored the saint's hierurgy; and men have beheld tears streaming from the eyes of venomous serpents when Ilar Agios uttered 'Curiluson' with a loud voice - since the serpent is not ignorant that by its wickedness sorrow came to the whole world. And when, in the time of the holy ministry, it is necessary that frequent Alleluyas should be chanted and vociferated, the saint wondered what should be done, for as yet none in that place was skilled in the art of song. Then was a great miracle, since from all the boughs of the wood, from every bush and from every green tree, there resounded Alleluyas in enchanting and prolonged harmony; never did the Bishop of Rome listen to so sweet a singing in his church as was heard in this wood. For the nightingale and thrush and blackbird and blackcap, and all their companions, are gathered together and sing praises to the Lord, chanting distinct notes and yet concluding in a melody of most ravishing sweetness; such was the mass of the Fisherman. Nor was this all, for one day as the saint prayed beside the well he became aware that a bee circled round and round his head, uttering loud buzzing sounds, but not endeavouring to sting him. To be short; the bee went before Ilar, and led him to a hollow tree not far off, and straightway a swarm of bees issued forth, leaving a vast store of wax behind them. This was their oblation to the Most High, for from their wax Ilar Sant made goodly candles to burn at the Offering; and from that time the bee is holy, because his wax makes light to shine upon the Gifts."

43

This was part of the story that Ambrose's father read to him; and they went again to see the Holy Well. He looked at the few broken and uneven stones that were left to distinguish it from common wells; and there in the deep green wood, in the summer afternoon, under the woven boughs, he seemed to hear the strange sound of the saint's bell, to see the woodland creatures hurrying through the undergrowth that they might be present at the Offering. The weasel beat his little breast for his sins; the big tears fell down the gentle face of the hare; the adders wept in the dust; and all the chorus of the birds sang: "Alleluya, Alleluya, Alleluya!"

Once they drove a long way from the Wern, going towards the west, till they came to the Great Mountain, as the people called it. After they had turned from the high road they went down a narrow lane, and this led them with many windings to a lower ridge of the mountain, where the horse and trap were put up at a solitary tavern. Then they began to toil upward on foot, crossing many glistening and rejoicing streams that rushed out cold from the limestone rock, mounting up and up, through the wet land where the rare orchis grew amongst the rushes, through hazel brakes, through fields that grew wilder as they still went higher, and the great wind came down from the high dome above them. They turned, and all the shining land was unrolled before them; the white houses were bright in the sunlight, and there, far away, was the yellow sea and the two islands, and the coasts beyond.

Nicholas Meyrick pointed out a tuft of trees on a hill a long way off and told his son that the Wern was hidden beyond it; and then they began to climb once more, till they came at last to the line where the fields and hedges ended, and above there was only the wild mountain land. And on this verge stood an old farmhouse with strong walls, set into the rock, sheltered a little from the winds by a line of twisted beeches. The walls of the house were gleaming white, and by the porch there was a shrub covered with bright yellow flowers. Mr. Meyrick beat upon the oak door, painted black and studded with heavy nails. An old man, dressed like a farmer, opened it, and Ambrose noticed that his father spoke to him with something of reverence in his voice, as if he were some very great person. They sat down in a long room, but dimly lighted by the thick greenish glass in the quarried window, and presently the old farmer set a great jug of beer before them. They both drank heartily enough, and Mr. Meyrick said:

"Aren't you about the last to brew your own beer, Mr. Cradock?"

"Iss; I be the last of all. They do all like the muck the brewer sends better than *cwrw dda*."

"The whole world likes muck better than good drink, now."

"You be right, Sir. Old days and old ways of our fathers, they be gone for ever. There was a blasted preacher down at the chapel a week or two ago, saying - so they do tell me - that they would all be damned to hell unless they took to ginger-beer directly. Iss indeed now; and I heard that he should say that a man could do a better day's work on that rot-belly stuff than on good beer. Wass you ever hear of such a liarr as that?"

The old man was furious at the thought of these infamies and follies; his esses hissed through his teeth and his r's rolled out with fierce emphasis. Mr. Meyrick nodded his approval of this indignation.

"We have what we deserve," he said. "False preachers, bad drink, the talk of fools all the day long - even on the mountain. What is it like, do you think, in London?"

There fell a silence in the long, dark room. They could hear the sound of the wind in the beech trees, and Ambrose saw how the boughs were tossed to and fro, and he thought of what it must be like in winter nights, here, high upon the Great Mountain, when the storms swept up from the sea, or descended from the wilds of the north; when the shafts of rain were like the onset of an army, and the winds screamed about the walls.

"May we see It?" said Mr. Meyrick suddenly.

"I did think you had come for that. There be very few now that remember."

He went out, and returned carrying a bunch of keys. Then he opened a door in the room and warned "the young master" to take care of the steps. Ambrose, indeed, could scarcely see the way. His father led him down a short flight of uneven stone steps, and they were in a room which seemed at first quite dark, for the only light came from a narrow window high up in the wall, and across the glass there were heavy iron bars.

Cradock lit two tall candles of yellow wax that stood in brass candlesticks on a table; and, as the flame grew clear, Ambrose saw that he was opening a sort of aumbry constructed in the thickness of the wall. The door was a great slab of solid oak, three or four inches thick - as one could see when it was opened - and from the dark place within the farmer took an iron box and set it carefully upon the floor, Mr. Meyrick helping him. They were strong men, but they staggered under the weight of the chest; the iron seemed as thick as the door of the cupboard from which it was taken, and the heavy, antique lock yielded, with a grating scream, to the key. Inside it there was another box of some reddish metal, which, again, held a case of wood black with age; and from this, with reverent hands, the farmer drew out a veiled and splendid cup and set it on the table between the two candles. It was a bowl-like vessel of the most wonderful workmanship, standing on a short stem. All the hues of the world were mingled on it, all the jewels of the regions seemed to shine from it; and the stem and foot were encrusted with work in enamel, of strange and magical colours that shone and dimmed with alternating radiance, that glowed with red fires and pale glories, with the blue of the far sky, the green of the faery seas, and the argent gleam of the evening star. But before Ambrose had gazed more than a moment he heard the old man say, in pure Welsh, not in broken English, in a resonant and chanting voice:

"Let us fall down and adore the marvellous and venerable work of the Lord God Almighty."

To which his father responded:

"Agyos, Agyos, Agyos. Mighty and glorious is the Lord God Almighty, in all His works and wonderful operations. Curiluson, Curiluson, Curiluson."

They knelt down, Cradock in the midst, before the cup, and Ambrose and his father on either hand. The holy vessel gleamed before the boy's eyes, and he saw clearly its wonder and its beauty. All its surface was a marvel of the most delicate intertwining lines in gold and silver, in copper and in bronze, in all manner of metals and alloys; and these interlacing patterns in their brightness, in the strangeness of their imagery and ornament, seemed to enthral his eyes and capture them, as it were, in a maze of enchantment; and not only the eyes; for the very spirit was rapt and garnered into that far bright world whence the holy magic of the cup proceeded. Among the precious stones which were set into the wonder was a great crystal, shining with the pure light of the moon; about the rim of it there was the appearance of faint and feathery clouds, but in the centre it was a white splendour; and as Ambrose gazed he thought that from the heart of this jewel there streamed continually a shower of glittering stars, dazzling his eyes with their incessant motion and brightness. His body thrilled with a sudden ineffable rapture, his breath came and went in quick pantings; bliss possessed him utterly as the three crowned forms passed in their golden order. Then the interwoven sorcery of the vessel became a ringing wood of golden, and bronze, and silver trees; from every side resounded the clear summons of the holy bells and the exultant song of the faery birds; he no longer heard the low-chanting voices of Cradock and his father as they replied to one another in the forms of some antique liturgy. Then he stood by a wild seashore; it was a dark night, and there was a shrilling wind that sang about the peaks of the sharp rock, answering to the deep voices of the heaving sea. A white moon, of fourteen days old, appeared for a moment in the rift between two vast black clouds, and the shaft of light showed all the savage desolation of the shore - cliffs that rose up into mountains, into crenellated heights that were incredible, whose bases were scourged by the torrents of hissing foam that were driven against them from the hollow-sounding sea. Then, on the highest of those awful heights, Ambrose became aware of walls and spires, of towers and battlements that must have touched the stars; and, in the midst of this great castle, there surged up the aspiring vault of a vast church, and all its windows were ablaze with a light so white and glorious that it was as if every pane were a diamond. And he heard the voices of a praising host, or the clamour of golden trumpets and the unceasing choir of the angels. And he knew that this place was the Sovereign Perpetual

Choir, Cor-arbennic, into whose secret the deadly flesh may scarcely enter. But in the vision he lay breathless, on the floor before the gleaming wall of the sanctuary, while the shadows of the hierurgy were enacted; and it seemed to him that, for a moment of time, he saw in unendurable light the Mystery of Mysteries pass veiled before him, and the Image of the Slain and Risen.

For a brief while this dream was broken. He heard his father singing softly:

"Gogoniant y Tâd ac y Mab ac yr Yspryd Glân."

And the old man answered:

"Agya Trias eleeson ymas."

Then again his spirit was lost in the bright depths of the crystal, and he saw the ships of the saints, without oar or sail, afloat on the faery sea, seeking the Glassy Isle. All the whole company of the Blessed Saints of the Isle of Britain sailed on the adventure; dawn and sunset, night and morning, their illuminated faces never wavered; and Ambrose thought that at last they saw bright shores in the dying light of a red sun, and there came to their nostrils the scent of the deep apple-garths in Avalon, and odours of Paradise.

When he finally returned to the presence of earthly things he was standing by his father; while Cradock reverently wrapped the cup in the gleaming veils which covered it, saying as he did so, in Welsh:

"Remain in peace, O holy and divine cup of the Lord. Henceforth I know not whether I shall return to thee or not; but may the Lord vouchsafe me to see thee in the Church of the Firstborn which is in Heaven, on the Altar of the Sacrifice which is from age unto ages."

Ambrose went up the steps and out into the sunshine on the mountain side with the bewilderment of strange dreams, as a coloured mist, about him. He saw the old white walls, the yellow blossoms by the porch; above, the wild, high mountain wall; and, below, all the dear land of Gwent, happy in the summer air, all its woods and fields, its rolling hills and its salt verge, rich in a golden peace. Beside him the cold water swelled from the earth and trickled from the grey rock, and high in the air an exultant lark was singing. The mountain breeze was full of life and gladness, and the rustling and tossing of the woods, the glint and glimmer of the leaves beneath, made one think that the trees, with every creature, were merry on that day. And in that dark cell beneath many locks, beneath wood and iron, concealed in golden, glittering veils, lay hidden that glorious and awful cup, glass of wonderful vision, portal and entrance of the Spiritual Place.

His father explained to him something of that which he had seen. He told him that the vessel was the Holy Cup of Teilo sant, which he was said to have received from the Lord in the state of Paradise, and that when Teilo said Mass, using that Chalice, the choir of angels was present visibly; that it was a cup of wonders and mysteries, the bestower of visions and heavenly graces.

"But whatever you do," he said, "do not speak to anyone of what you have seen to-day, because if you do the mystery will be laughed at and blasphemed. Do you know that your uncle and aunt at Lupton would say that we were all mad together? That is because they are fools, and in these days most people are fools, and malignant fools too, as you will find out for yourself before you are much older. So always remember that you must hide the secrets that you have seen; and if you do not do so you will be sorry."

Mr. Meyrick told his son why old Cradock was to be treated with respect - indeed, with reverence.

"He is just what he looks," he said, "an old farmer with a small freehold up here on the mountain side; and, as you heard, his English is no better than that of any other farmer in this country. And, compared with Cradock, the Duke of Norfolk is a man of yesterday. He is of the tribe of Teilo the Saint; he is the last, in direct descent, of the hereditary keepers of the holy cup; and his race has guarded that blessed relic for thirteen hundred years. Remember, again, that to-day, on this mountain, you have seen great marvels which you must keep in silence."

Poor Ambrose! He suffered afterwards for his forgetfulness of his father's injunction. Soon after he went to Lupton one of the boys was astonishing his friends with a brilliant account of the Crown jewels, which he had viewed during the Christmas holidays. Everybody was deeply impressed, and young Meyrick, anxious to be agreeable in his turn, began to tell about the wonderful cup that he had once seen in an old farmhouse. Perhaps his manner was not convincing, for the boys shrieked with laughter over his description. A monitor who was passing asked to hear the joke, and, having been told the tale, clouted Ambrose over the head for an infernal young liar. This was a good lesson, and it served Ambrose in good stead when one of the masters having, somehow or other, heard the story, congratulated him in the most approved scholastic manner before the whole form on his wonderful imaginative gifts.

"I see the budding novelist in you, Meyrick," said this sly master. "Besant and Rice will be nowhere when you once begin. I suppose you are studying character just at present? Let us down gently, won't you? [To the delighted form.] We must be careful, mustn't we, how we behave? 'A chiel's amang us takin' notes,'" etc. etc.

But Meyrick held his tongue. He did not tell his form master that he was a beast, a fool and a coward, since he had found out that the truth, like many precious things, must often be concealed from the profane. A late vengeance overtook that foolish master. Long years after, he was dining at a popular London restaurant, and all through dinner he had delighted the ladies of his party by the artful mixture of brutal insolence and vulgar chaff with which he had treated one of the waiters, a humble-looking little Italian. The master was in the highest spirits at the success of his persiflage; his voice rose louder and louder, and his offensiveness became almost supernaturally acute. And then he received a heavy earthen casserole, six quails, a few small onions and a quantity of savoury but boiling juices full in the face. The waiter was a Neapolitan.

The hours of the night passed on, as Ambrose sat in his bedroom at the Old Grange, recalling many wonderful memories, dreaming his dreams of the mysteries, of the land of Gwent and the land of vision, just as his uncle, but a few yards away in another room of the house, was at the same time rapt into the world of imagination, seeing the new Lupton descending like a bride from the heaven of headmasters. But Ambrose thought of the Great Mountain, of the secret valleys, of the sanctuaries and hallows of the saints, of the rich carven work of lonely churches hidden amongst the hills and woods. There came into his mind the fragment of an old poem which he loved:

In the darkness of old age let not my memory fail,
Let me not forget to celebrate the beloved land of Gwent.
If they imprison me in a deep place, in a house of pestilence,
Still shall I be free, when I remember the sunshine upon Mynydd Maen.
There have I listened to the singing of the lark, my soul has ascended with the song of the little bird;
The great white clouds were the ships of my spirit, sailing to the haven of the Almighty.
Equally to be held in honour is the site of the Great Mountain,
Adorned with the gushing of many waters -
Sweet is the shade of its hazel thickets,
There a treasure is preserved, which I will not celebrate,
It is glorious, and deeply concealed.
If Teilo should return, if happiness were restored to the Cymri,
Dewi and Dyfrig should serve his Mass; then a great marvel would be made visible.
O blessed and miraculous work, then should my bliss be as the bliss of angels;
I had rather behold this Offering than kiss the twin lips of dark Gwenllian.
Dear my land of Gwent, O quam dilecta tabernacula!
Thy rivers are like precious golden streams of Paradise,
Thy hills are as the Mount Syon -
Better a grave on Twyn Barlwm than a throne in the palace of the Saxons at Caer-Ludd.

And then, by the face of contrast, he thought of the first verse of the great school song, "Rocker," one of the earliest of the many poems which his uncle had consecrated to the praise of the dear old school:

Once on a time, in the books that bore me,
I read that in olden days before me
Lupton town had a wonderful game,
It was a game with a noble story
(Lupton town was then in its glory,
Kings and Bishops had brought it fame).
It was a game that you all must know,
And 'rocker' they called it, long ago.

Chorus.

Look out for 'brooks,' or you're sure to drown,
Look out for 'quarries,' or else you're down -
That was the way 'Rocker' to play -
Once on a day That was the way, Once on a day,
That was the way that they used to play in Lupton town.

Thinking of the two songs, he put out his light and, wearied, fell into a deep sleep.

IV

The British schoolboy, considered in a genial light by those who have made him their special study, has not been found to be either observant or imaginative. Or, rather, it would be well to say that his powers of observation, having been highly specialised within a certain limited tract of thought and experience (bounded mainly by cricket and football), are but faint without these bounds; while it is one of the chiefest works of the System to kill, destroy, smash and bring to nothing any powers of imagination he may have originally possessed. For if this were not done thoroughly, neither a Conservative nor a Liberal administration would be possible, the House of Commons itself would cease to exist, the Episcopus (var. Anglicanus) would go the way of the Great Bustard; a "muddling through somehow" (which must have been *the* brightest jewel in the British crown, wrung from King John by the barons) would become a lost art. And, since all these consequences would be clearly intolerable, the great Public Schools have perfected a very thorough system of destroying the imaginative toxin, and few cases of failure have been so far reported.

Still, there are facts which not even the densest dullards, the most complete boobies, can help seeing; and a good many of the boys found themselves wondering "what was the matter with Meyrick" when they saw him at Chapel on the Sunday morning. The news of his astounding violences both of act and word on the night before had not yet circulated generally. Bates was attending to that department, but hadn't had time to do much so far; and the replies of Pelly and Rawson to enquiries after black eyes and a potato-like nose were surly and misleading. Afterwards, when the tale was told, when Bates, having enlarged the incidents to folk-lore size, showed Pelly lying in a pool of his own blood, Rawson screaming as with the torments of the lost and Meyrick rolling out oaths - all original and all terrible - for the space of a quarter of an hour, then indeed the school was satisfied; it was no wonder if Meyrick did look a bit queer after the achievement of such an adventure. The funk of aforetime had found courage; the air of rapture was easily understood. It is probable that if, in the nature of things, it had been possible for an English schoolboy to meet St. Francis of Assisi, the boy would have concluded that the saint must have just made 200 not out in first-class cricket.

But Ambrose walked in a strange light; he had been admitted into worlds undreamed of, and from the first brightness of the sun, when he awoke in the morning in his room at the Grange, it was the material world about him, the walls of stone and brick, the solid earth, the sky itself, and the people who talked and moved and seemed alive - these were things of vision, unsubstantial shapes, odd and broken illusions of the mind. At half-past seven old Toby, the man-of-all-work at the old Grange banged at his door and let his clean boots fall with a crash on the boards after the usual fashion. He awoke, sat up in bed, staring about him. But what was this? The four walls covered with a foolish speckled paper, pale blue and pale brown, the white ceiling, the bare boards with the strip of carpet by the bedside: he knew nothing of all this. He was not horrified, because he knew that it was all non-existent, some plastic fantasy that happened to be presented for the moment to his brain. Even the big black wooden chest that held his books (*Parker*, despised by Horbury, among them) failed to appeal to him with any sense of reality; and the bird's-eye washstand and chest of drawers, the white water-jug with the blue band, were all frankly phantasmal. It reminded him of a trick he had sometimes played: one chose one's position carefully, shut an eye and, behold, a mean shed could be made to obscure the view of a mountain! So these walls and appurtenances made an illusory sort of intrusion into the true vision on which he gazed. That yellow washstand rising out of the shining wells of the undying, the speckled walls in the place of the great mysteries, a chest of drawers in the magic garden of roses - it had the air of a queer joke, and he laughed aloud to himself as he realized that he alone knew, that everybody else would say, "That is a white jug with a blue band," while he, and he only, saw the marvel and glory of the holy cup with its glowing metals, its interlacing myriad lines, its wonderful images, and its hues of the mountain and the stars, of the green wood and the faery sea where, in a sure haven, anchor the ships that are bound for Avalon.

For he had a certain faith that he had found the earthly presentation and sacrament of the Eternal Heavenly Mystery.

He smiled again, with the quaint smile of an angel in an old Italian picture, as he realized more fully the strangeness of the whole position and the odd humours which would relieve to play a wonderful game of make-believe; the speckled walls, for instance, were not really there, but he was to behave just as if they were solid realities. He would presently rise and go through an odd pantomine of washing and dressing, putting on brilliant boots, and going down to various mumbo-jumbo ceremonies called breakfast, chapel and dinner, in the company of appearances to whom he would accord all the honours due to veritable beings. And this delicious phantasmagoria would go on and on day after day, he alone having the secret; and what a delight it would be to "play up" at rocker! It seemed to him that the solid-seeming earth, the dear old school and rocker itself had all been made to minister to the acuteness of his pleasure; they were the darkness that made the light visible, the matter through which form was manifested. For the moment he enclosed in the most secret place of his soul the true world into which he had been guided; and as he dressed he hummed the favourite school song, "Never mind!"

> *If the umpire calls 'out' at your poor second over,*
> *If none of your hits ever turns out a 'rover,'*
> *If you fumble your fives and 'go rot' over sticker,*
> *If every hound is a little bit quicker;*
> *If you can't tackle rocker at all, not at all,*
> *And kick at the moon when you try for the ball,*
> *Never mind, never mind, never mind - if you fall,*
> *Dick falls before rising,*
> *Tom's short ere he's tall,*
> *Never mind!*
> *Don't be one of the weakest who go to the wall:*
> *Never mind!*

Ambrose could not understand how Columbus could have blundered so grossly. Somehow or other he should have contrived to rid himself of his crew; he should have returned alone, with a dismal tale of failure, and passed the rest of his days as that sad and sorry charlatan who had misled the world with his mad whimsies of a continent beyond the waters of the Atlantic. If he had been given wisdom to do this, how great - how wonderful would his joys have been! They would have pointed at him as he paced the streets in his shabby cloak; the boys would have sung songs about him and his madness; the great people would have laughed contemptuously as he went by. And he would have seen in his heart all that vast far world of the west, the rich islands barred by roaring surf, a whole hemisphere of strange regions and strange people; he would have known that he alone possessed the secret of it. But, after all, Ambrose knew that his was a greater joy even than this; for the world that he had discovered was not far across the seas, but within him.

Pelly stared straight before him in savage silence all through breakfast; he was convinced that mere hazard had guided that crushing blow, and he was meditating schemes of complete and exemplary vengeance. He noticed nothing strange about Meyrick, nor would he have cared if he had seen the images of the fairies in his eyes. Rawson, on the other hand, was full of genial civility and good fellowship; it was "old chap" and "old fellow" every other word. But he was far from unintelligent, and, as he slyly watched Meyrick, he saw that there was something altogether unaccustomed and incomprehensible. Unknown lights burned and shone in the eyes, reflections of one knew not what; the expression was altered in some queer way that he could not understand. Meyrick had always been a rather ugly, dogged-looking fellow; his black hair and something that was not usual in the set of his features gave him an exotic, almost an Oriental appearance; hence a story of Rawson's to the effect that Meyrick's mother was a nigger woman in poor circumstances and of indifferent morality had struck the school as plausible enough.

But now the grimness of the rugged features seemed abolished; the face shone, as it were, with the light of a flame - but a flame of what fire? Rawson, who would not have put his observations into such terms, drew his own conclusions readily enough and imparted them to Pelly after Chapel.

"Look here, old chap," he said, "did you notice young Meyrick at breakfast?"

Pelly simply blasted Meyrick and announced his intention of giving him the worst thrashing he had ever had at an early date.

"Don't you try it on," said Rawson. "I had my eye on him all the time. He didn't see I was spotting him. He's cracked; he's dangerous. I shouldn't wonder if he were in a strait waistcoat in the County Lunatic Asylum in a week's time. My governor had a lot to do with lunatics, and he always says he can tell by the eyes. I'll swear Meyrick is raging mad."

"Oh, rot!" said Pelly. "What do you know about it?"

"Well, look out, old chap, and don't say I didn't give you the tip. Of course, you know a maniac is stronger than three ordinary men? The only thing is to get them down and crack their ribs. But you want at least half a dozen men before you can do it."

"Oh, shut up!"

So Rawson said no more, remaining quite sure that he had diagnosed Ambrose's symptoms correctly. He waited for the catastrophe with a dreadful joy, wondering whether Meyrick would begin by cutting old Horbury's throat with his own razor, or whether he would rather steal into Pelly's room at night and tear him limb from limb, a feat which, as a madman, he could, of course, accomplish with perfect ease. As a matter of fact, neither of these events happened. Pelly, a boy of the bulldog breed, smacked Ambrose's face a day or two later before a huge crowd of boys, and received in return such a terrific blow under the left ear that a formal fight in the Tom Brown manner was out of the question.

Pelly reached the ground and stayed there in an unconscious state for some while; and the other boys determined that it would be as well to leave Meyrick to himself. He might be cracked but he was undoubtedly a hard hitter. As for Pelly, like the sensible fellow that he was, he simply concluded that Meyrick was too good for him. He did not quite understand it; he dimly suspected the intrusion of some strange forces, but with such things he had nothing to do. It was a fair knock-out, and there was an end of it.

Bates had glanced up as Ambrose came into the dining-room on the Sunday morning. He saw the shining face, the rapturous eyes, and had silently wondered, recognising the presence of elements which transcended all his calculations.

Meanwhile the Lupton Sunday went on after its customary fashion. At eleven o'clock the Chapel was full of boys. There were nearly six hundred of them there, the big ones in frock-coats, with high, pointed collars, which made them look like youthful Gladstones. The younger boys wore broad, turn-down collars and had short, square jackets made somewhat in the Basque fashion. Young and old had their hair cut close to the scalp, and this gave them all a brisk but bullety appearance. The masters, in cassock, gown and hood, occupied the choir stalls. Mr. Horbury, the High Usher, clothed in a flowing surplice, was taking Morning Prayer, and the Head occupied a kind of throne by the altar.

The Chapel was not an inspiring building. It was the fourteenth century, certainly, but the fourteenth century translated by 1840, and, it is to be feared, sadly betrayed by the translators. The tracery of the windows was poor and shallow; the mouldings of the piers and arches faulty to a degree; the chancel was absurdly out of proportion, and the pitch-pine benches and stalls had a sticky look. There was a stained-glass window in memory of the Old Luptonians who fell in the Crimea. One wondered what the Woman of Samaria by the Well had to do either with Lupton or the Crimea. And the colouring was like that used in very common, cheap sweets.

The service went with a rush. The prayers, versicles and responses, and psalms were said, the officiant and the congregation rather pressing than pausing - often, indeed, coming so swiftly to cues that two or three words at the end of one verse or two or three at the beginning of the next would be lost in a confused noise of contending voices. But *Venite* and *Te Deum* and *Benedictus* were rattled off to frisky Anglicans with great spirit; sometimes the organ tooted, sometimes it bleated gently, like a flock of sheep; now one might have sworn that the music of penny whistles stole on the ear, and again, as the organist coupled up the full organ, using suddenly all the battery of his stops, a gas explosion and a Salvation Army band seemed to strive against one another. A well-known nobleman who had been to Chapel at Lupton was heard to say, with reference to this experience: "I am no Ritualist, heaven knows - but I confess I like a hearty service."

But it was, above all, the sermon that has made the Chapel a place of many memories. The Old Boys say - and one supposes that they are in earnest - that the tall, dignified figure of the Doctor, standing high above them all, his scarlet hood making a brilliant splash of colour against the dingy, bilious paint of the pale green walls, has been an inspiration to them in all quarters of the globe, in all manner of difficulties and temptations.

One man writes that in the midst of a complicated and dangerous deal on the Stock Exchange he remembered a sermon of Dr. Chesson's called in the printed volume, "Fighting the Good Fight."

"You have a phrase amongst you which I often hear," said the Head. "That phrase is 'Play the game,' and I wish to say that, though you know it not; though, it may be, the words are often spoken half in jest; still, they are but your modern, boyish rendering of the old, stirring message which I have just read to you.

"Fight the Good Fight.' 'Play the Game.' Remember the words in the storm and struggle, the anxiety and stress that may be - nay, must be - before you - etc., etc., etc."

"After the crisis was over," wrote the Stock Exchange man, "I was thankful that I *had* remembered those words."

"That voice sounding like a trumpet on the battle-field, bidding us all remember that Success was the prize of Effort and Endurance - - " So writes a well-known journalist.

"I remembered what the Doctor said to us once about 'running the race,'" says a young soldier, recounting a narrow escape from a fierce enemy, "so I stuck to my orders."

Ambrose, on that Sunday morning, sat in his place, relishing acutely all the savours of the scene, consumed with inward mirth at the thought that this also professed to be a rite of religion. There was an aimless and flighty merriment about the chant to the *Te Deum* that made it difficult for him to control his laughter; and when he joined in the hymn "Pleasant are Thy courts above," there was an odd choke in his voice that made the boy next to him shuffle uneasily.

But the sermon!

It will be found on page 125 of the *Lupton Sermons*. It dealt with the Parable of the Talents, and showed the boys in what the sin of the man who concealed his Talent really consisted.

"I daresay," said the Head, "that many of the older amongst you have wondered what this man's sin really was. You may have read your Greek Testaments carefully, and then have tried to form in your minds some analogy to the circumstances of the parable - and it would not surprise me if you were to tell me that you had failed.

"What manner of man was this? I can imagine your saying one to another. I shall not be astonished if you confess that, for you at least, the question seems unanswerable.

"Yes; Unanswerable to you. For you are English boys, the sons of English gentlemen, to whom the atmosphere of casuistry, of concealment, of subtlety, is unknown; by whom such an atmosphere would be rejected with scorn. You come from homes where there is no shadow, no dark corner which must not be pried into. Your relations and your friends are not of those who hide their gifts from the light of day. Some of you, perhaps, have had the privilege of listening to the talk of one or other of the great statesmen who guide the doctrines of this vast Empire. You will have observed, I am sure, that in the world of politics there is no vain simulation of modesty, no feigned reluctance to speak of worthy achievement. All of you are members of this great community, of which each one of us is so proud, which we think of as the great inspiration and motive force of our lives. Here, you will say, there are no Hidden Talents, for the note of the English Public School (thank God for it!) is openness, frankness, healthy emulation; each endeavouring to do his best for the good of all. In our studies and in our games each desires to excel to carry off the prize. We strive for a corruptible crown, thinking that this, after all, is the surest discipline for the crown that is incorruptible. If a man say that he loveth God whom he hath not seen, and love not his brother whom he hath seen! Let your light *shine* before men. Be sure that we shall never win Heaven by despising earth.

"Yet that man hid his Talent in a napkin. What does the story mean? What message has it for us to-day?

"I will tell you.

"Some years ago during our summer holidays I was on a walking tour in a mountainous district in the north of England. The sky was of a most brilliant blue, the sun poured, as it were, a gospel of gladness on the earth. Towards the close of the day I was entering a peaceful and beautiful valley amongst the hills, when three sullen notes of a bell came down the breeze towards me. There was a pause. Again the three strokes, and for a third time this dismal summons struck my ears. I walked on in the direction of the sound, wondering whence it came and what it signified; and soon I saw before me a great pile of buildings, surrounded by a gloomy and lofty wall.

"It was a Roman Catholic monastery. The bell was ringing the Angelus, as it is called.

"I obtained admittance to this place and spoke to some of the unhappy monks. I should astonish you if I mentioned the names of some of the deluded men who had immured themselves in this prison-house. It is sufficient to say that among them were a soldier who had won distinction on the battle-field, an artist, a statesman and a physician of no mean repute.

"Now do you understand? Ah! a day will come - you know, I think, what that day is called - when these poor men will have to answer the question: 'Where is the Talent that was given to you?'

"'Where was your sword in the hour of your country's danger?'

"'Where was your picture, your consecration of your art to the service of morality and humanity, when the doors of the great Exhibition were thrown open?'

"'Where was your silver eloquence, your voice of persuasion, when the strife of party was at its fiercest?'

"'Where was your God-given skill in healing when One of Royal Blood lay fainting on the bed of dire - almost mortal - sickness?'

"And the answer? 'I laid it up in a napkin.' And now, etc., etc."

Then the whole six hundred boys sang "O Paradise! O Paradise!" with a fervour and sincerity that were irresistible. The organ thundered till the bad glass shivered and rattled, and the service was over.

V

Almost the last words that Ambrose had heard after his wonderful awaking were odd enough, though at the time he took little note of them, since they were uttered amidst passionate embraces, amidst soft kisses on his poor beaten flesh. Indeed, if these words recurred to him afterwards, they never made much impression on his mind, though to most people they would seem of more serious import than much else that was uttered that night! The sentences ran something like this:

"The cruel, wicked brute! He shall be sorry all his days, and every blow shall be a grief to him. My dear! I promise you he shall pay for to-night ten times over. His heart shall ache for it till it stops beating."

There cannot be much doubt that this promise was kept to the letter. No one knew how wicked rumours concerning Mr. Horbury got abroad in Lupton, but from that very day the execution of the sentence began. In the evening the High Usher, paying a visit to a friend in town, took a short cut through certain dark, ill-lighted streets, and was suddenly horrified to hear his name shrieked out, coupled with a most disgusting accusation. His heart sank down in his breast; his face, he knew, was bloodless; and then he rushed forward to the malpassage whence the voice seemed to proceed.

There was nothing there. It was a horrid little alley, leading from one slum to another, between low walls and waste back-gardens, dismal and lampless. Horbury ran at top speed to the end of it, but there was nothing to be done. A few women were gossiping at their doors, a couple of men slouched past on their way to the beer-shop at the corner - that was all. He asked one of the women if she had seen anybody running, and she said no, civilly enough - and yet he fancied that she had leered at him.

He turned and went back home. He was not in the mood for paying visits. It was some time before he could compose his mind by assuring himself that the incident, though unpleasant, was not of the slightest significance. But from that day the nets were about his feet, and his fate was sealed.

Personally, he was subjected to no further annoyance, and soon forgot that unpleasant experience in the back-street. But it seems certain that from that Sunday onwards a cloud of calumny overshadowed the High Usher in all his ways. No one said anything definite, but everyone appeared to be conscious of something unpleasant when Horbury's name was mentioned. People looked oddly at one another, and the subject was changed.

One of the young masters, speaking to a colleague, did indeed allude casually to Horbury as Xanthias Phoceus. The other master, a middle-aged man, raised his eyebrows and shook his head without speaking. It is understood that these muttered slanders were various in their nature; but, as has been said, everything was indefinite, intangible as contagion - and as deadly to the master's worldly health.

That horrible accusation which had been screamed out of the alley was credited by some; others agreed with the young master; while a few had a terrible story of an idiot girl in a remote Derbyshire village. And the persistence of all these fables was strange.

It was four years before Henry Vibart Chesson, D. D., ascended the throne of St. Guthmund at Dorchester; and all through those four years the fountain of evil innuendo rose without ceasing. It is doubtful how far belief in the truth of these scandals was firm and settled, or how far they were in the main uttered and circulated by ill-natured people who disliked Horbury, but did not in their hearts believe him guilty of worse sins than pompousness and arrogance. The latter is the more probable opinion.

Of course, the deliberations of the Trustees were absolutely secret, and the report that the Chairman, the Marquis of Dunham, said something about Cæsar's wife is a report and nothing more. It is evident that the London press was absolutely in the dark as to the existence of this strange conspiracy of vengeance, since two of the chief dailies took the appointment of the High Usher to the Headmastership as a foregone conclusion, prophesying, indeed, a rule of phenomenal success. And then Millward, a Winchester man, understood to be rather unsound on some scholastic matters - "not *quite* the right man"; "just a *little* bit of a Jesuit" - received the appointment, and people did begin to say that there must be a screw loose somewhere. And Horbury was overwhelmed, and began to die.

The odd thing was that, save on that Sunday night, he never saw the enemy; he never suspected that there was an enemy; And as for the incident of the alley, after a little consideration he treated it with contempt. It was only some drunken beast in the town who knew him by sight and wished to be offensive, in the usual fashion of drunken beasts.

And there was nothing else. Lupton society was much too careful to allow its suspicions to be known. A libel action meant, anyhow, a hideous scandal and might have no pleasant results for the libellers. Besides, no one wanted to offend Horbury, who was suspected of possessing a revengeful temper; and it had not dawned on the Lupton mind that the rumours they themselves were circulating would eventually ruin the High Usher's chances of the Headmastership. Each gossip heard, as it were, only his own mutter at the moment. He did not realize that when a great many people are muttering all at once an ugly noise of considerable volume is being produced.

It is true that a few of the masters were somewhat cold in their manner. They lacked the social gift of dissimulation, and could not help showing their want of cordiality. But Horbury, who noticed this, put it down to envy and disaffection, and resolved that the large powers given him by the Trustees should not be in vain so far as the masters in question were concerned.

Indeed, C. L. Wood, who was afterwards Headmaster of Marcester and died in Egypt a few years ago, had a curious story which in part relates to the masters in question, and perhaps throws some light on the extraordinary tale of Horbury's ruin.

Wood was an old Luptonian. He was a mighty athlete in his time, and his records for the Long Jump and Throwing the Cricket Ball have not been beaten at Lupton to this day. He had been one of the first boarders taken at the Old Grange. The early relations between Horbury and himself had been continued in later life, and Wood was staying with his former master at the time when the Trustee's decision was announced. It is supposed, indeed, that Horbury had offered him a kind of unofficial, but still important, position in the New Model; in fact, Wood confessed over his port that the idea was that he should be a kind of "Intelligence Department" to the Head. He did not seem very clear as to the exact scope of his proposed duties. We may certainly infer, however, that they would have been of a very confidential nature, for Wood had jotted down his recollections of that fatal morning somewhat as follows:

"I never saw Horbury in better spirits. Indeed, I remember thinking that he was younger than ever - younger than he was in the old days when he was a junior master and I was in the Third. Of course, he was always energetic; one could not disassociate the two notions of Horbury and energy, and I used to make him laugh by threatening to include the two terms in the new edition of my little book, *Latin and English Synonyms*. It did not matter whether he were taking the Fifth, or editing Classics for his boys, or playing rocker - one could not help rejoicing in the vivid and ebullient energy of the man. And perhaps this is one reason why shirkers and loafers dreaded him, as they certainly did.

"But during those last few days at Lupton his vitality had struck me as quite superhuman. As all the world knows, his succession to the Headmastership was regarded by everyone as assured, and he was, naturally and properly, full of the great task which he believed was before him. This is not the place to argue the merits or demerits of the scheme which had been maturing for many years in his brain.

"A few persons who, I cannot but think, have received very imperfect information on the subject, have denounced Horbury's views of the modern Public School as revolutionary. Revolutionary they certainly were, as an express engine is revolutionary compared to an ox-waggon. But those who think of the late Canon Horbury as indifferent to the good side of Public School traditions knew little of the real man. However, were his plans good or bad, they were certainly of vast scope, and on the first night of my visit he made me sit up with him till two o'clock while he expounded his ideas, some of which, as he was good enough to say, he trusted to me to carry out. He showed me the piles of MS. he had accumulated: hundreds of pages relating to the multiple departments of the great organisation which he was to direct, or rather to create; sheets of serried figures, sheaves of estimates which he had caused to be made out in readiness for immediate action.

"Nothing was neglected. I remember seeing a note on the desirability of compiling a 'Lupton Hymn Book' for use in the Chapel, and another on the question of forming a Botanical Garden, so that the school botany might be learned from 'the green life,' as he beautifully expressed it, not from dry letterpress and indifferent woodcuts. Then, I think, on a corner of the 'Botany Leaf' was a jotting - a mere hasty scrawl, waiting development and consideration: 'Should we teach Hindustani? Write to Tucker re the Moulvie Ahmed Khan.'

"I despair of giving the reader any conception of the range and minuteness of these wonderful memoranda. I remember saying to Horbury that he seemed to be able to use the microscope and the telescope at the same time. He laughed joyously, and told me to wait till he was really at work. 'You will have your share, I promise you,' he added. His high spirits were extraordinary and infectious. He was an excellent *raconteur*, and now and again, amidst his talk of the New Lupton which he was about to translate from the idea into substance, he told some wonderful stories which I have not the heart to set down here. *Tu ne quæsieris*. I have often thought of those lines when I remember Horbury's intense happiness, the nervous energy which made the delay of a day or two seem almost intolerable. His brain and his fingers tingled, as it were, to set about the great work before him. He reminded me of a mighty host, awaiting but the glance of their general to rush forward with irresistible force.

"There was not a trace of misgiving. Indeed, I should have been utterly astonished if I had seen anything of the kind. He told me, indeed, that for some time past he had suspected the existence of a sort of cabal or clique against him. 'A. and X., B. and Y., M. and N., and, I think, Z., are in it,' he said, naming several of the masters. 'They are jealous, I suppose, and want to make things as difficult as they can. They are all cowards, though, and I don't believe one of them - except, perhaps, M. - would fail in obedience, or rather in subservience, when it comes to the point. But I am going to make short work of the lot.' And he told me his intention of ridding the school of these disaffected elements. 'The Trustees will back me up, I know,' he added, 'but we must try to avoid all unnecessary friction'; and he explained to me a plan he had thought of for eliminating the masters in question. 'It won't do to have half-hearted officers on our ship,' was the way in which he put it, and I cordially agreed with him.

"Possibly he may have underrated the force of the opposition which he treated so lightly; possibly he altogether misjudged the situation. He certainly regarded the appointment as already made, and this, of course, was, or appeared to be, the conviction of all who knew anything of Lupton and Horbury.

"I shall never forget the day on which the news came. Horbury made a hearty breakfast, opening letters, jotting down notes, talking of his plans as the meal proceeded. I left him for a while. I was myself a good deal excited, and I strolled up and down the beautiful garden at the Old Grange, wondering whether I should be able to satisfy such a chief who, the soul of energy himself, would naturally expect a like quality in his subordinates. I rejoined him in the course of an hour in the study, where he was as busy as ever - 'snowed up,' as he expressed it, in a vast pile of papers and correspondence.

"He nodded genially and pointed to a chair, and a few minutes later a servant came in with a letter. She had just found it in the hall, she explained. I had taken a book and was reading. I noticed nothing till what I can only call a groan of intense anguish made me look up in amazement - indeed, in horror - and I was shocked to see my old friend, his face a ghastly white, his eyes staring into vacancy, and his expression one of the most terrible - *the* most terrible - that I have ever witnessed. I cannot describe that look. There was an agony of grief and despair, a glance of the wildest amazement, terror, as of an impending awful death, and with these the fiercest and most burning anger that I have ever seen on any human face. He held a letter clenched in his hand. I was afraid to speak or move.

"It was fully five minutes before he regained his self-control, and he did this with an effort which was in itself dreadful to contemplate - so severe was the struggle. He explained to me in a voice which faltered and trembled with the shock that he had received, that he had had very bad news - that a large sum of money which was absolutely necessary to the carrying out of his projects had been embezzled by some unscrupulous person, that he did not know what he should do. He fell back into his chair; in a few minutes he had become an old man.

"He did not seem upset, or even astonished, when, later in the day, a telegram announced that he had failed in the aim of his life - that a stranger was to bear rule in his beloved Lupton. He murmured something to the effect that it was no matter now. He never held up his head again."

This note is an extract from *George Horbury: a Memoir*. It was written by Dr. Wood for the use of a few friends and privately printed in a small edition of a hundred and fifty copies. The author felt, as he explains in his brief *Foreword,* that by restricting the sale to those who either knew Horbury or were especially interested in his work, he was enabled to dwell somewhat intimately on matters which could hardly have been treated in a book meant for the general public.

The extract that has been made from this book is interesting on two points. It shows that Horbury was quite unaware of what had been going on for four years before Chesson's resignation and that he had entirely misinterpreted the few and faint omens which had been offered him. He was preparing to break a sulky sentinel or two when all the ground of his fortalice was a very network of loaded mines! The other point is still more curious. It will be seen from Wood's story that the terrific effect that he describes was produced by a letter, received some hours before the news of the Trustees' decision arrived by telegram. "Later in the day" is the phrase in the Memoir; as a matter of fact, the final deliberation of the Lupton Trustees, held at Marshall's Hotel in Albemarle Street, began at eleven-thirty and was not over till one-forty-five. It is not likely that the result could have reached the Old Grange before two-fifteen; whereas the letter found in the hall must have been read by Horbury before ten o'clock. The invariable breakfast hour at the Old Grange was eight o'clock.

C. L. Wood says: "I rejoined him in the course of an hour," and the letter was brought in "a few minutes later." Afterwards, when the fatal telegram arrived, the Memoir notes that the unfortunate man was not "even astonished." It seems to follow almost necessarily from these facts that Horbury learnt the story of his ruin from the letter, for it has been ascertained that the High Usher's account of the contents of the letter was false from beginning to end. Horbury's most excellent and sagacious investments were all in the impeccable hands of "Witham's" (Messrs. Witham, Venables, Davenport and Witham), of Raymond Buildings, Gray's Inn, who do not include embezzlement in their theory and practice of the law; and, as a matter of fact, the nephew, Charles Horbury, came into a very handsome fortune on the death of his uncle - eighty thousand pounds in personality, with the Old Grange and some valuable ground rents in the new part of Lupton. It is as certain as anything can be that George Horbury never lost a penny by embezzlement or, indeed, in any other way.

One may surmise, then, the real contents of that terrible letter. In general, that is, for it is impossible to conjecture whether the writer told the whole story; one does not know, for example, whether Meyrick's name was mentioned or not: whether there was anything which carried the reader's mind to that dark evening in November when he beat the white-faced boy with such savage cruelty. But from Dr. Wood's description of the wretched man's appearance one understands how utterly unexpected was the crushing blow that had fallen upon him. It was a lightning flash from the sky at its bluest, and before that sudden and awful blast his whole life fell into deadly and evil ruin.

"He never held up his head again." He never lived again, one may say, unless a ceaseless wheel of anguish and anger and bitter and unavailing and furious regret can be called life. It was not a man, but a shell, full of gall and fire, that went to Wareham; but probably he was not the first of the Klippoth to be made a Canon.

As we have no means of knowing exactly what or how much that letter told him, one is not in a position to say whether he recognised the singularity - one might almost say, the eccentricity - with which his punishment was stage-managed. *Nec deus intersit* certainly; but a principle may be pushed too far, and a critic might point out that, putting avenging deities in their machines on one side, it was rather going to the other extreme to bring about the Great Catastrophe by means of bad sherry, a trying Headmaster, boiled mutton, a troublesome schoolboy and a servant-maid. Yet these were the agents employed; and it seems that we are forced to the conclusion that we do not altogether understand the management of the universe. The conclusion is a dangerous one, since we may be led by it, unless great care is exercised, into the worst errors of the Dark Ages.

There is the question, of course, of the truthfulness or falsity of the various slanders which had such a tremendous effect. The worst of them were lies - there can be little doubt of that - and for the rest, it may be hinted that the allusion of the young master to Xanthias Phoceus was not very far wide of the mark. Mrs. Horbury had been dead some years, and it is to be feared that there had been passages between the High Usher and Nelly Foran which public opinion would have condemned. It would be difficult to tell the whole story, but the girl's fury of revenge makes one apt to believe that she was exacting payment not only for Ambrose's wrongs, but for some grievous injury done to herself.

But before all these things could be brought to their ending, Ambrose Meyrick had to live in wonders and delights, to be initiated in many mysteries, to discover the meaning of that voice which seemed to speak within him, denouncing him because he had pried unworthily into the Secret which is hidden from the Holy Angels.

CHAPTER III

I

One of Ambrose Meyrick's favourite books was a railway timetable. He spent many hours in studying these intricate pages of figures, noting times of arrival and departure on a piece of paper, and following the turnings and intersections of certain lines on the map. In this way he had at last arrived at the best and quickest route to his native country, which he had not seen for five years. His father had died when he was ten years old.

This result once obtained, the seven-thirty to Birmingham got him in at nine-thirty-five; the ten-twenty for the west was a capital train, and he would see the great dome of Mynydd Mawr before one o'clock. His fancy led him often to a bridge which crossed the railway about a mile out of Lupton. East and west the metals stretched in a straight line, defying, it seemed, the wisdom of Euclid. He turned from the east and gazed westward, and when a red train went by in the right direction he would lean over the bridge and watch till the last flying carriage had vanished into the distance. He imagined himself in that train and thought of the joy of it, if the time ever came - for it seemed long - the joy in every revolution of the wheels, in every whistle of the engine; in the rush and in the rhythm of this swift flight from that horrible school and that horrible place.

Year after year went by and he had not revisited the old land of his father. He was left alone in the great empty house in charge of the servants during the holidays - except one summer when Mr. Horbury despatched him to a cousin of his who lived at Yarmouth.

The second year after his father's death there was a summer of dreadful heat. Day after day the sky was a glare of fire, and in these abhorred Midlands, far from the breath of the sea and the mountain breeze, the ground baked and cracked and stank to heaven. A dun smoke rose from the earth with the faint, sickening stench of a brick-field, and the hedgerows swooned in the heat and in the dust. Ambrose's body and soul were athirst with the desire of the hills and the woods; his heart cried out within him for the waterpools in the shadow of the forest; and in his ears continually he heard the cold water pouring and trickling and dripping from the grey rocks on the great mountain side. And he saw that awful land which God has no doubt made for manufacturers to prepare them for their eternal habitation, its weary waves burning under the glaring sky: the factory chimneys of Lupton vomiting their foul smoke; the mean red streets, each little hellway with its own stink; the dull road, choking in its dust. For streams there was the Wand, running like black oil between black banks, steaming here as boiling poisons were belched into it from the factory wall; there glittering with iridescent scum vomited from some other scoundrel's castle. And for the waterpools of the woods he was free to gaze at the dark green liquor in the tanks of the Sulphuric Acid factory, but a little way out of town. Lupton was a very rising place.

His body was faint with the burning heat and the foulness of all about him, and his soul was sick with loneliness and friendlessness and unutterable longing. He had already mastered his Bradshaw and had found out the bridge over the railway; and day after day he leaned over the parapet and watched the burning metals vanishing into the west, into the hot, thick haze that hung over all the land. And the trains sped away towards the haven of his desire, and he wondered if he should ever see again the dearly loved country or hear the song of the nightingale in the still white morning, in the circle of the green hills. The thought of his father, of the old days of happiness, of the grey home in the still valley, swelled in his heart and he wept bitterly, so utterly forsaken and wretched seemed his life.

It happened towards the end of that dreadful August that one night he had tossed all through the hours listening to the chiming bells, only falling into a fevered doze a little while before they called him. He woke from ugly and oppressive dreams to utter wretchedness; he crawled downstairs like an old man and left his breakfast untouched, for he could eat nothing. The flame of the sun seemed to burn in his brain; the hot smoke of the air choked him. All his limbs ached. From head to foot he was a body of suffering. He struggled out and tottered along the road to the bridge and gazed with dim, hopeless eyes along the path of desire, into the heavy, burning mist in the far distance. And then his heart beat quick, and he cried aloud in his amazed delight; for, in the shimmering glamour of the haze, he saw as in a mirror the vast green wall of the Great Mountain rise before him - not far, but as if close at hand. Nay, he stood upon its slope; his feet were in the sweet-smelling bracken; the hazel thicket was rustling beneath him in the brave wind, and the shining water poured cold from the stony rock. He heard the silver note of the lark, shrilling high and glad in the sunlight. He saw the yellow blossoms tossed by the breeze about the porch of the white house. He seemed to turn in this vision and before him the dear, long-remembered land appeared in its great peace and beauty: meadows and cornfield, hill and valley and deep wood between the mountains and the far sea. He drew a long breath of that quickening and glorious air, and knew that life had returned to him. And then he was gazing once more down the glittering railway into the mist; but strength and hope had replaced that deadly sickness of a moment before, and light and joy came back to his eyes.

The vision had doubtless been given to him in his sore and pressing need. It returned no more; not again did he see the fair height of Mynydd Mawr rise out of the mist. But from that day the station on the bridge was daily consecrated. It was his place of refreshment and hope in many seasons of evil and weariness.

From this place he could look forward to the hour of release and return that must come at last. Here he could remind himself that the bonds of the flesh had been broken in a wonderful manner; that he had been set free from the jaws of hell and death.

Fortunately, few people came that way. It was but a by-road serving a few farms in the neighbourhood, and on the Sunday afternoon, in November, the Head's sermon over and dinner eaten, he betook himself to his tower, free to be alone for a couple of hours, at least.

He stood there, leaning on the wall, his face turned, as ever, to the west, and, as it were, a great flood of rapture overwhelmed him. He sank down, deeper, still deeper, into the hidden and marvellous places of delight. In his country there were stories of the magic people who rose all gleaming from the pools in lonely woods; who gave more than mortal bliss to those who loved them; who could tell the secrets of that land where flame was the most material substance; whose inhabitants dwelt in palpitating and quivering colours or in the notes of a wonderful melody. And in the dark of the night all legends had been fulfilled.

It was a strange thing, but Ambrose Meyrick, though he was a public schoolboy of fifteen, had lived all his days in a rapt innocence. It is possible that in school, as elsewhere, enlightenment, pleasant or unpleasant, only comes to those who seek for it - or one may say certainly that there are those who dwell under the protection of enchantments, who may go down into the black depths and yet appear resurgent and shining, without any stain or defilement of the pitch on their white robes. For these have ears so intent on certain immortal songs that they cannot hear discordant voices; their eyes are veiled with a light that shuts out the vision of evil. There are flames about these feet that extinguish the gross fires of the pit.

It is probable that all through those early years Ambrose's father had been charming his son's heart, drawing him forth from the gehenna-valley of this life into which he had fallen, as one draws forth a beast that has fallen into some deep and dreadful place. Various are the methods recommended. There is the way of what is called moral teaching, the way of physiology and the way of a masterly silence; but Mr. Meyrick's was the strange way of incantation. He had, in a certain manner, drawn the boy aside from that evil traffic of the valley, from the stench of the turmoil, from the blows and the black lechery, from the ugly fight in the poisonous smoke, from all the amazing and hideous folly that practical men call life, and had set him in that endless procession that for ever and for ever sings its litanies in the mountains, going from height to height on its great quest. Ambrose's soul had been caught in the sweet thickets of the woods; it had been bathed in the pure water of blessed fountains; it had knelt before the altars of the old saints, till all the earth was become a sanctuary, all life was a rite and ceremony, the end of which was the attainment of the mystic sanctity - the achieving of the Graal. For this - for what else? - were all things made. It was this that the little bird sang of in the bush, piping a few feeble, plaintive notes of dusky evenings, as if his tiny heart were sad that it could utter nothing better than such sorry praises. This also celebrated the awe of the white morning on the hills, the breath of the woods at dawn. This was figured in the red ceremony of sunset, when flames shone over the dome of the great mountain, and roses blossomed in the far plains of the sky. This was the secret of the dark places in the heart of the woods. This the mystery of the sunlight on the height; and every little flower, every delicate fern, and every reed and rush was entrusted with the hidden declaration of this sacrament. For this end, final and perfect rites had been given to men to execute; and these were all the arts, all the far-lifted splendour of the great cathedral; all rich carven work and all glowing colours; all magical utterance of word and tones: all these things were the witnesses that consented in the One Offering, in the high service of the Graal.

To this service also, together with songs and burning torches and dyed garments and the smoke of the bruised incense, were brought the incense of the bruised heart, the magic torches of virtue hidden from the world, the red dalmatics of those whose souls had been martyred, the songs of triumph and exultation chanted by them that the profane had crushed into the dust; holy wells and water-stoups were fountains of tears. So must the Mass be duly celebrated in Cor-arbennic when Cadwaladr returned, when Teilo Agyos lifted up again the Shining Cup.

Perhaps it was not strange that a boy who had listened to such spells as these should heed nothing of the foolish evils about him, the nastiness of silly children who, for want of wits, were "crushing the lilies into the dunghill." He listened to nothing of their ugly folly; he heard it not, understood it not, thought as little of it as of their everlasting chatter about "brooks" and "quarries" and "leg-hits" and "beaks from the off." And when an unseemly phrase did chance to fall on his ear it was of no more import or meaning than any or all of the stupid jargon that went on day after day, mixing itself with the other jargon about the optative and the past participle, the oratio obliqua and the verbs in [Greek: mi]. To him this was all one nothingness, and he would not have dreamed of connecting anything of it with the facts of life, as he understood life.

Hence it was that for him all that was beautiful and wonderful was a part of sanctity; all the glory of life was for the service of the sanctuary, and when one saw a lovely flower it was to be strewn before the altar, just as the bee was holy because by its wax the Gifts are illuminated. Where joy and delight and beauty were, there he knew by sure signs were the parts of the mystery, the glorious apparels of the heavenly vestments. If anyone had told him that the song of the nightingale was an unclean thing he would have stared in amazement, as though one had blasphemed the Sanctus. To him the red roses were as holy as the garments of the martyrs. The white lilies were pure and shining virtues; the imagery of the *Song of Songs* was obvious and perfect and unassailable, for in this world there was nothing common nor unclean. And even to him the great gift had been freely given.

So he stood, wrapt in his meditations and in his ecstasy, by the bridge over the Midland line from Lupton to Birmingham. Behind him were the abominations of Lupton: the chimneys vomiting black smoke faintly in honour of the Sabbath; the red lines of the workmen's streets advancing into the ugly fields; the fuming pottery kilns, the hideous height of the boot factory. And before him stretched the unspeakable scenery of the eastern Midlands, which seems made for the habitation of English Nonconformists - dull, monotonous, squalid, the very hedgerows cropped and trimmed, the trees looking like rows of Roundheads, the farmhouses as uninteresting as suburban villas. On a field near at hand a scientific farmer had recently applied an agreeable mixture consisting of superphosphate of lime, nitrate of soda and bone meal. The stink was that of a chemical works or a Texel cheese. Another field was just being converted into an orchard. There were rows of grim young apple trees planted at strictly mathematical intervals from one another, and grisly little graves had been dug between the apple trees for the reception of gooseberry bushes. Between these rows the farmer hoped to grow potatoes, so the ground had been thoroughly trenched. It looked sodden and unpleasant. To the right Ambrose could see how the operations on a wandering brook were progressing. It had moved in and out in the most wasteful and absurd manner, and on each bank there had grown a twisted brake of trees and bushes and rank water plants. There were wonderful red roses there in summer time. Now all this was being rectified. In the first place the stream had been cut into a straight channel with raw, bare banks, and then the rose bushes, the alders, the willows and the rest were being grubbed up by the roots and so much valuable land was being redeemed. The old barn which used to be visible on the left of the line had been pulled down for more than a year. It had dated perhaps from the seventeenth century. Its roof-tree had dipped and waved in a pleasant fashion, and the red tiles had the glow of the sun in their colours, and the half-timbered walls were not lacking in ruinous brace. It was a dilapidated old shed, and a neat-looking structure with a corrugated iron roof now stood in its place.

Beyond all was the grey prison wall of the horizon; but Ambrose no longer gazed at it with the dim, hopeless eyes of old. He had a Breviary among his books, and he thought of the words: *Anima mea erepta est sicut passer de laqueo venantium*, and he knew that in a good season his body would escape also. The exile would end at last.

He remembered an old tale which his father was fond of telling him - the story of Eos Amherawdur (the Emperor Nightingale). Very long ago, the story began, the greatest and the finest court in all the realms of faery was the court of the Emperor Eos, who was above all the kings of the Tylwydd Têg, as the Emperor of Rome is head over all the kings of the earth. So that even Gwyn ap Nudd, whom they now call lord over all the fair folk of the Isle of Britain, was but the man of Eos, and no splendour such as his was ever seen in all the regions of enchantment and faery. Eos had his court in a vast forest, called Wentwood, in the deepest depths of the green-wood between Caerwent and Caermaen, which is also called the City of the Legions; though some men say that we should rather name it the city of the Waterfloods. Here, then, was the Palace of Eos, built of the finest stones after the Roman manner, and within it were the most glorious chambers that eye has ever seen, and there was no end to the number of them, for they could not be counted. For the stones of the palace being immortal, they were at the pleasure of the Emperor. If he had willed, all the hosts of the world could stand in his greatest hall, and, if he had willed, not so much as an ant could enter into it, since it could not be discerned. But on common days they spread the Emperor's banquet in nine great halls, each nine times larger than any that are in the lands of the men of Normandi. And Sir Caw was the seneschal who marshalled the feast; and if you would count those under his command - go, count the drops of water that are in the Uske River. But if you would learn the splendour of this castle it is an easy matter, for Eos hung the walls of it with Dawn and Sunset. He lit it with the sun and moon. There was a well in it called Ocean. And nine churches of twisted boughs were set apart in which Eos might hear Mass; and when his clerks sang before him all the jewels rose shining out of the earth, and all the stars bent shining down from heaven, so enchanting was the melody. Then was great bliss in all the regions of the fair folk. But Eos was grieved because mortal ears could not hear nor comprehend the enchantment of their song. What, then, did he do? Nothing less than this. He divested himself of all his glories and of his kingdom, and transformed himself into the shape of a little brown bird, and went flying about the woods, desirous of teaching men the sweetness of the faery melody. And all the other birds said: "This is a contemptible stranger." The eagle found him not even worthy to be a prey; the raven and the magpie called him simpleton; the pheasant asked where he had got that ugly livery; the lark wondered why he hid himself in the darkness of the wood; the peacock would not suffer his name to be uttered. In short never was anyone so despised as was Eos by all the chorus of the birds. But wise men heard that song from the faery regions and listened all night beneath the bough, and these were the first who were bards in the Isle of Britain.

Ambrose had heard the song from the faery regions. He had heard it in swift whispers at his ear, in sighs upon his breast, in the breath of kisses on his lips. Never was he numbered amongst the despisers of Eos.

II

Mr. Horbury had suffered from one or two slight twinges of conscience for a few days after he had operated on his nephew. They were but very slight pangs, for, after all, it was a case of flagrant and repeated disobedience to rules, complicated by lying. The High Usher was quite sincere in scouting the notion of a boy's taking any interest in Norman architecture, and, as he said to himself, truly enough, if every boy at Lupton could come and go when and how he pleased, and choose which rules he would keep and which disobey - why, the school would soon be in a pretty state. Still, there was a very faint and indistinct murmur in his mind which suggested that Meyrick had received, in addition to his own proper thrashing, the thrashings due to the Head, his cook and his wine merchant. And Horbury was rather sorry, for he desired to be just according to his definition of justice - unless, indeed justice should be excessively inconvenient.

But these faint scruples were soon removed - turned, indeed, to satisfaction by the evident improvement which declared itself in Ambrose Meyrick's whole tone and demeanour. He no longer did his best to avoid rocker. He played, and played well and with relish. The boy was evidently all right at heart: he had only wanted a sharp lesson, and it was clear that, once a loafer, he was now on his way to be a credit to the school. And by some of those secret channels which are known to masters and to masters alone, rather more than a glimmering of the truth as to Rawson's black eyes and Pelly's disfigured nose was vouchsafed to Horbury's vision, and he was by no means displeased with his nephew. The two boys had evidently asked for punishment, and had got it. It served them right. Of course, if the swearing had been brought to his notice by official instead of by subterranean and mystic ways, he would have had to cane Meyrick a second time, since, by the Public School convention, an oath is a very serious offence - as bad as smoking, or worse; but, being far from a fool, under the circumstances he made nothing of it. Then the lad's school work was so very satisfactory. It had always been good, but it had become wonderfully good. That last Greek prose had shown real grip of the language. The High Usher was pleased. His sharp lesson had brought forth excellent results, and he foresaw the day when he would be proud of having taught a remarkably fine scholar.

With the boys Ambrose was becoming a general favourite. He learned not only to play rocker, he showed Pelly how he thought that blow under the ear should be dealt with. They all said he was a good fellow; but they could not make out why, without apparent reason, he would sometimes burst out into loud laughter. But he said it was something wrong with his inside - the doctors couldn't make it out - and this seemed rather interesting.

In after life he often looked back upon this period when, to all appearance, Lupton was "making a man" of him, and wondered at its strangeness. To boys and masters alike he was an absolutely normal schoolboy, busy with the same interests as the rest of them. There was certainly something rather queer in his appearance; but, as they said, generously enough, a fellow couldn't help his looks; and, that curious glint in the eyes apart, he seemed as good a Luptonian as any in the whole six hundred. Everybody thought that he had absolutely fallen into line; that he was absorbing the ethos of the place in the most admirable fashion, subduing his own individuality, his opinions, his habits, to the general tone of the community around him - putting off, as it were, the profane dust of his own spirit and putting on the mental frock of the brotherhood. This, of course, is one of the aims - rather, *the* great aim - of the system: this fashioning of very diverse characters into one common form, so that each great Public School has its type, which is easily recognisable in the grown-up man years after his school days are over. Thus, in far lands, in India and Egypt, in Canada and New Zealand, one recognises the brisk alertness of the Etonian, the exquisite politeness of Harrow, the profound seriousness of Rugby; while the note of Lupton may, perhaps, be called finality. The Old Luptonian no more thinks of arguing a question than does the Holy Father, and his conversation is a series of irreformable dogmas, and the captious person who questions any one article is made to feel himself a cad and an outsider.

Thus it has been related that two men who had met for the first time at a certain country house-party were getting on together capitally in the evening over their whisky and soda and cigars. Each held identical views of equal violence on some important topic - Home Rule or the Transvaal or Free Trade - and, as the more masterful of the two asserted that hanging was too good for Blank (naming a well-known statesman), the other would reply: "I quite agree with you: hanging is too good for Blank."

"He ought to be burned alive," said the one.

"That's about it: he ought to be burned at the stake," answered the other.

"Look at the way he treated Dash! He's a coward and a damned scoundrel!"

"Perfectly right. He's a damned cursed scoundrel!"

This was splendid, and each thought the other a charming companion. Unfortunately, however, the conversation, by some caprice, veered from the iniquities of Blank and glanced aside to cookery - possibly by the track of Irish stew, used metaphorically to express the disastrous and iniquitous policy of the great statesman with regard to Ireland. But, as it happened, there was not the same coincidence on the question of cookery as there had been on the question of Blank. The masterful man said:

"No cookery like English. No other race in the world can cook as we do. Look at French cookery - a lot of filthy, greasy messes."

Now, instead of assenting briskly and firmly as before the other man said: "Been much in France? Lived there?"

"Never set foot in the beastly country! Don't like their ways, and don't care to dine off snails and frogs swimming in oil."

The other man began then to talk of the simple but excellent meals he had relished in France - the savoury *croûte-au-pot*, the *bouilli* - good eating when flavoured by a gherkin or two; velvety *épinards au jus*, a roast partridge, a salad, a bit of Roquefort and a bunch of grapes. But he had barely mentioned the soup when the masterful one wheeled round his chair and offered a fine view of his strong, well-knit figure - as seen from the back. He did not say anything - he simply took up the paper and went on smoking. The other men stared in amazement: the amateur of French cookery looked annoyed. But the host - a keen-eyed old fellow with a white moustache, turned to the enemy of frogs and snails and grease and said quite simply: "I say, Mulock, I never knew you'd been at Lupton."

Mulock gazed. The other men held their breath for a moment as the full force of the situation dawned on them, and then a wild scream of laughter shrilled from their throats. Yells and roars of mirth resounded in the room. Their delight was insatiable. It died for a moment for lack of breath, and then burst out anew in still louder, more uproarious clamour, till old Sir Henry Rawnsley, who was fat and short, could do nothing but choke and gasp and crow out a sound something between a wheeze and a chuckle. Mulock left the room immediately, and the house the next morning. He made some excuse to his host, but he told enquiring friends that, personally, he disliked bounders.

The story, true or false, illustrates the common view of the Lupton stamp.

"We try to teach the boys to know their own minds," said the Headmaster, and the endeavour seems to have succeeded in most cases. And, as Horbury noted in an article he once wrote on the Public School system, every boy was expected to submit himself to the process, to form and reform himself in accordance with the tone of the school.

"I sometimes compare our work with that of the metal founder," he says in the article in question. "Just as the metal comes to the foundry *rudis indigestaque moles*, a rough and formless mass, without the slightest suggestion of the shape which it must finally assume, so a boy comes to a great Public School with little or nothing about him to suggest the young man who, in eight or nine years' time, will say good-bye to the dear old school, setting his teeth tight, restraining himself from giving up to the anguish of this last farewell. Nay, I think that ours is the harder task, for the metal that is sent to the foundry has, I presume, been freed of its impurities; we have to deal rather with the ore - a mass which is not only shapeless, but contains much that is not metal at all, which must be burnt out and cast aside as useless rubbish. So the boy comes from his home, which may or may not have possessed valuable formative influences; which we often find has tended to create a spirit of individualism and assertiveness; which, in numerous cases, has left the boy under the delusion that he has come into the world to live his own life and think his own thoughts. This is the ore that we cast into our furnace. We burn out the dross and rubbish; we liquefy the stubborn and resisting metal till it can be run into the mould - the mould being the whole tone and feeling of a great community. We discourage all excessive individuality; we make it quite plain to the boy that he has come to Lupton, not to live his life, not to think his thoughts, but to live *our* life, to think *our* thoughts. Very often, as I think I need scarcely say, the process is a somewhat unpleasant one, but, sooner or later, the stubbornest metal yields to the cleansing, renewing, restoring fires of discipline and public opinion, and the shapeless mass takes on the shape of the Great School. Only the other day an old pupil came to see me and confessed that, for the whole of his first year at Lupton, he had been profoundly wretched. 'I was a dreamy young fool,' he said. 'My head was stuffed with all sorts of queer fancies, and I expect that if I hadn't come to Lupton I should have turned out an absolute loafer. But I hated it badly that first year. I loathed rocker - I did, really - and I thought the fellows were a lot of savages. And then I seemed to go into a kind of cloud. You see, Sir, I was losing my old self and hadn't got the new self in its place, and I couldn't make out what was happening. And then, quite suddenly, it all came out light and clear. I saw the purpose behind it all - how we were all working together, masters and boys, for the dear old school; how we were all "members one of another," as the Doctor said in Chapel; and that I had a part in this great work, too, though I was only a kid in the Third. It was like a flash of light: one minute I was only a poor little chap that nobody cared for and who didn't matter to anybody, and the next I saw that, in a way, I was as important as the Doctor himself - I was a part of the failure or success of it all. Do you know what I did, Sir? I had a book I thought a lot of - *Poems and Tales* of Edgar Allan Poe. It was my poor sister's book; she had died a year before when she was only seventeen, and she had written my name in it when she was dying - she knew I was fond of reading it. It was just the sort of thing I used to like - morbid fancies and queer poems, and I was always reading it when the fellows would let me alone. But when I saw what life really was, when the meaning of it all came to me, as I said just now, I took that book and tore it to bits, and it was like tearing myself up. But I knew that writing all that stuff hadn't done that American fellow much good, and I didn't see what good I should get by reading it. I couldn't make out to myself that it would fit in with the Doctor's plans of the spirit of the school, or that I should play up at rocker any better for knowing all about the "Fall of the House of Usher," or whatever it's called. I knew my poor sister would understand, so I tore it up, and I've gone straight ahead ever since - thanks to Lupton.' *Like a refiner's fire.* I remembered the dreamy, absent-minded child of fifteen years before; I could scarcely believe that he stood before - keen, alert, practical, living every moment of his life, a force, a power in the world, certain of successful achievement."

Such were the influences to which Ambrose Meyrick was being subjected, and with infinite success, as it seemed to everybody who watched him. He was regarded as a conspicuous instance of the efficacy of the system - he had held out so long, refusing to absorb the "tone," presenting an obstinate surface to the millstones which would, for his own good, have ground him to powder, not concealing very much his dislike of the place and of the people in it. And suddenly he had submitted with a good grace: it was wonderful! The masters are believed to have discussed the affair amongst themselves, and Horbury, who confessed or boasted that he had used sharp persuasion, got a good deal of *kudos* in consequence.

III

A few years ago a little book called *Half-holidays* attracted some attention in semi-scholastic, semi-clerical circles. It was anonymous, and bore the modest motto *Crambe bis cocta*; but those behind the scenes recognised it as the work of Charles Palmer, who was for many years a master at Lupton. His acknowledged books include a useful little work on the Accents and an excellent summary of Roman History from the Fall of the Republic to Romulus Augustulus. The *Half-holidays* contains the following amusing passage; there is not much difficulty in identifying the N. mentioned in it with Ambrose Meyrick.

"The cleverest dominie sometimes discovers" - the passage begins - "that he has been living in a fool's paradise, that he has been tricked by a quiet and persistent subtlety that really strikes one as almost devilish when one finds it exhibited in the person of an English schoolboy. A good deal of nonsense, I think, has been written about boys by people who in reality know very little about them; they have been credited with complexities of character, with feelings and aspirations and delicacies of sentiment which are quite foreign to their nature. I can quite believe in the dead cat trick of Stalky and his friends, but I confess that the incident of the British Flag leaves me cold and sceptical. Such refinement of perception is not the way of the boy - certainly not of the boy as I have known him. He is radically a simple soul, whose feelings are on the surface; and his deepest laid schemes and manœuvres hardly call for the talents of a Sherlock Holmes if they are to be detected and brought to naught. Of course, a good deal of rubbish has been talked about the wonderful success of our English plan of leaving the boys to themselves without the everlasting supervision which is practised in French schools. As a matter of fact, the English schoolboy is under constant supervision; where in a French school one wretched usher has to look after a whole horde of boys, in an English school each boy is perpetually under the observation of hundreds of his fellows. In reality, each boy is an unpaid *pion*, a watchdog whose vigilance never relaxes. He is not aware of this; one need scarcely say that such a notion is far from his wildest thoughts. He thinks, and very rightly, doubtless, that he is engaged in maintaining the honour of the school, in keeping up the observance of the school tradition, in dealing sharply with slackers and loafers who would bring discredit on the place he loves so well. He is, no doubt, absolutely right in all this; none the less, he is doing the master's work unwittingly and admirably. When one thinks of this, and of the Compulsory System of Games, which ensures that every boy shall be in a certain place at a certain time, one sees, I think, that the phrase about our lack of supervision *is* a phrase and nothing more. There is no system of supervision known to human wit that approaches in thoroughness and minuteness the supervision under which every single boy is kept all through his life at an English Public School.

"Hence one is really rather surprised when, in spite of all these unpaid assistants, who are the whole school, one is thoroughly and completely taken in. I can only remember one such case, and I am still astonished at the really infernal ability with which the boy in question lived a double life under the very eyes of the masters and six hundred other boys. N., as I shall call him, was not in my House, and I can scarcely say how I came to watch his career with so much interest; but there was certainly something about him which did interest me a good deal. It may have been his appearance: he was an odd-looking boy - dark, almost swarthy, dreamy and absent in manner, and, for the first years of his school life, a quite typical loafer. Such boys, of course, are not common in a big school, but there are a few such everywhere. One never knows whether this kind will write a successful book, or paint a great picture, or go to the devil - from my observation I am sorry to say that the last career is the most usual. I need scarcely say that such boys meet with but little encouragement; it is not the type which the Public School exists to foster, and the boy who abandons himself to morbid introspection is soon made to feel pretty emphatically that he is matter in the wrong place. Of course, one may be crushing genius. If this ever happened it would be very unfortunate; still, in all communities the minority must suffer for the good of the majority, and, frankly, I have always been willing to run the risk. As I have hinted, the particular sort of boy I have in my mind turns out in nine cases out of ten to be not a genius, but that much more common type - a blackguard.

"Well, as I say, I was curious about N. I was sorry for him, too; both his parents were dead, and he was rather in the position of the poor fellows who have no home life to look forward to when the holidays are getting near. And his obstinacy astonished me; in most cases the pressure of public opinion will bring the slackest loafer to a sense of the error of his ways before his first term is ended; but N. seemed to hold out against us all with a sort of dreamy resistance that was most exasperating. I do not think he can have had a very pleasant time. His general demeanour suggested that of a sage who has been cast on an island inhabited by a peculiarly repulsive and degraded tribe of savages, and

I need scarcely say that the other boys did their best to make him realise the extreme absurdity of such behaviour. He was clever enough at his work, but it was difficult to make him play games, and impossible to make him play up. He seemed to be looking through us at something else; and neither the boys nor the masters liked being treated as unimportant illusions. And then, quite suddenly, N. altered completely. I believe his housemaster, worn out of all patience, gave him a severe thrashing; at any rate, the change was instant and marvellous.

"I remember that a few days before N.'s transformation we had been discussing the question of the cane at the weekly masters' meeting. I had confessed myself a very half-hearted believer in the efficacy of the treatment. I forget the arguments that I used, but I know that I was strongly inclined to favour the 'Anti-baculist Party,' as the Head jocosely named it. But a few months later when N.'s housemaster pointed out N. playing up at football like a young demon, and then with a twinkle in his eye reminded me of the position I had taken up at the masters' meeting, there was nothing for it but to own that I had been in the wrong. The cane had certainly, in this case, proved itself a magic wand; the sometime loafer had been transformed by it into one of the healthiest and most energetic fellows in the whole school. It was a pleasure to watch him at the games, and I remember that his fast bowling was at once terrific in speed and peculiarly deadly in its accuracy.

"He kept up this deception, for deception it was, for three or four years. He was just going up to Oxford, and the whole school was looking forward to a career which we knew would be quite exceptional in its brilliance. His scholarship papers astonished the Balliol authorities. I remember one of the Fellows writing to our Head about them in terms of the greatest enthusiasm, and we all knew that N.'s bowling would get him into the University Eleven in his first term. Cricketers have not yet forgotten a certain performance of his at the Oval, when, as a poetic journalist observed, wickets fell before him as ripe corn falls before the sickle. N. disappeared in the middle of term. The whole school was in a ferment; masters and boys looked at one another with wild faces; search parties were sent out to scour the country; the police were communicated with; on every side one heard the strangest surmises as to what had happened. The affair got into the papers; most people thought it was a case of breakdown and loss of memory from overwork and mental strain. Nothing could be heard of N., till, at the end of a fortnight, his Housemaster came into our room looking, as I thought, puzzled and frightened.

"'I don't understand,' he said. 'I've had this by the second post. It's in N.'s handwriting. I can't make head or tail of it. It's some sort of French, I suppose.'

"He held out a paper closely written in N.'s exquisite, curious script, which always reminded me vaguely of some Oriental character. The masters shook their heads as the manuscript went from hand to hand, and one of them suggested sending for the French master. But, as it happened, I was something of a student of Old French myself, and I found I could make out the drift of the document that N. had sent his master.

"It was written in the manner and in the language of Rabelais. It was quite diabolically clever, and beyond all question the filthiest thing I have ever read. The writer had really exceeded his master in obscenity, impossible as that might seem: the purport of it all was a kind of nightmare vision of the school, the masters and the boys. Everybody and everything were distorted in the most horrible manner, seen, we might say, through an abominable glass, and yet every feature was easily recognisable; it reminded me of Swift's disgusting description of the Yahoos, over which one may shudder and grow sick, but which one cannot affect to misunderstand. There was a fantastic episode which I remember especially. One of us, an ambitious man, who for some reason or other had become unpopular with a few of his colleagues, was described as endeavouring to climb the school clock-tower, on the top of which a certain object was said to be placed. The object was defended, so the writer affirmed, by 'the Dark Birds of Night,' who resisted the master's approach in all possible and impossible manners. Even to indicate the way in which this extraordinary theme was treated would be utterly out of the question; but I shall never forget the description of the master's face, turned up towards the object of his quest, as he painfully climbed the wall. I have never read even in the most filthy pages of Rabelais, or in the savagest passages of Swift, anything which approached the revolting cruelty of those few lines. They were compounded of hell-fire and the *Cloaca Maxima*.

"I read out and translated a few of the least abominable sentences. I can hardly say whether the feeling of disgust or that of bewilderment predominated amongst us. One of my colleagues stopped me and said they had heard enough; we stared at one another in silence. The astounding ability, ferocity and obscenity of the whole thing left us quite dumbfounded, and I remember saying that if a volcano were suddenly to belch forth volumes of flame and filth in the middle of the playing fields I should scarcely be more astonished. And all this was the work of N., whose brilliant abilities in games and in the schools were to have been worth many thousands a year to X., as one of us put it! This was the boy that for the last four years we had considered as a great example of the formative influences of the school! This was the N. who we thought would have died for the honour of the school, who spoke as if he could never do enough to repay what X. had done for him! As I say, we looked at one another with faces of blank amazement and horror. At last somebody said that N. must have gone mad, and we tried to believe that it was so, for madness, awful calamity as it is, would be more endurable than sanity under such circumstances as these. I need scarcely say that this charitable hypothesis turned out to be quite unfounded: N. was perfectly sane; he was simply revenging himself for the suppression of his true feelings for the four last years of his school life. The 'conversion' on which we prided ourselves had been an utter sham; the whole of his life had been an elaborately organised hypocrisy maintained with unfailing and unflinching skill term after term and year after year. One cannot help wondering when one considers the inner life of this unhappy fellow. Every morning, I suppose, he woke up with curses in his soul; he smiled at us all and joined in the games with black rage devouring him. So far as one can say, he was quite sincere in his concealed opinions at all events. The hatred, loathing and contempt of the whole system of the place displayed in that extraordinary and terrible document struck me as quite genuine; and while I was reading it I could not help thinking of his eager, enthusiastic face as he joined with a will in the school songs; he seemed to inspire all the boys about him with something of his own energy and devotion. The apparition was a shocking one; I felt that for a moment I had caught a glimpse of a region that was very like hell itself.

"I remember that the French master contributed a characteristic touch of his own. Of course, the Headmaster had to be told of the matter, and it was arranged that M. and myself should collaborate in the unpleasant task of making a translation. M. read the horrible stuff through with an expression on his face that, to my astonishment, bordered on admiration, and when he laid down the paper he said:

"'*Eh bien: Maître François est encore en vie, évidemment. C'est le vrai renouveau de la Renaissance; de la Renaissance en très mauvaise humeur, si vous voulez, mais de la Renaissance tout-de-même. Si, si; c'est de la crû véritable, je vous assure. Mais, notre bon N. est un Rabelais qui a habité une terre affreusement sèche.'*

"I really think that to the Frenchman the terrible moral aspect of the case was either entirely negligible or absolutely non-existent; he simply looked on N.'s detestable and filthy performance as a little masterpiece in a particular literary genre. Heaven knows! One does not want to be a Pharisee; but as I saw M. grinning appreciatively over this dung-heap I could not help feeling that the collapse of France before Germany offered no insoluble problem to the historian.

"There is little more to be said as to this extraordinary and most unpleasant affair. It was all hushed up as much as possible. No further attempts to discover N.'s whereabouts were made. It was some months before we heard by indirect means that the wretched fellow had abandoned the Balliol Scholarship and the most brilliant prospects in life to attach himself to a company of greasy barnstormers - or 'Dramatic Artists,' as I suppose they would be called nowadays. I believe that his subsequent career has been of a piece with these beginnings; but of that I desire to say nothing."

The passage has been quoted merely in evidence of the great success with which Ambrose Meyrick adapted himself to his environment at Lupton. Palmer, the writer, who was a very well-meaning though intensely stupid person, has told the bare facts as he saw them accurately enough; it need not be said that his inferences and deductions from the facts are invariably ridiculous. He was a well-educated man; but in his heart of hearts he thought that Rabelais, *Maria Monk, Gay Life in Paris and La Terre* all came to much the same thing.

IV

In an old notebook kept by Ambrose Meyrick in those long-past days there are some curious entries which throw light on the extraordinary experiences that befell him during the period which poor Palmer has done his best to illustrate. The following is interesting:

"I told her she must not come again for a long time. She was astonished and asked me why - was I not fond of her? I said it was because I was so fond of her, that I was afraid that if I saw her often I could not live. I should pass away in delight because our bodies are not meant to live for long in the middle of white fire. I was lying on my bed and she stood beside it. I looked up at her. The room was very dark and still. I could only just see her faintly, though she was so close to me that I could hear her breathing quite well. I thought of the white flowers that grew in the dark corners of the old garden at the Wern, by the great ilex tree. I used to go out on summer nights when the air was still and all the sky cloudy. One could hear the brook just a little, down beyond the watery meadow, and all the woods and hills were dim. One could not see the mountain at all. But I liked to stand by the wall and look into the darkest place, and in a little time those flowers would seem to grow out of the shadow. I could just see the white glimmer of them. She looked like the flowers to me, as I lay on the bed in my dark room.

"Sometimes I dream of wonderful things. It is just at the moment when one wakes up; one cannot say where one has been or what was so wonderful, but you know that you have lost everything in waking. For just that moment you knew everything and understood the stars and the hills and night and day and the woods and the old songs. They were all within you, and you were all light. But the light was music, and the music was violet wine in a great cup of gold, and the wine in the golden cup was the scent of a June night. I understood all this as she stood beside my bed in the dark and stretched out her hand and touched me on the breast.

"I knew a pool in an old, old grey wood a few miles from the Wern. I called it the grey wood because the trees were ancient oaks that they say must have grown there for a thousand years, and they have grown bare and terrible. Most of them are all hollow inside and some have only a few boughs left, and every year, they say, one leaf less grows on every bough. In the books they are called the Foresters' Oaks. If you stay under them you feel as if the old times must have come again. Among these trees there was a great yew, far older than the oaks, and beneath it a dark and shadowy pool. I had been for a long walk, nearly to the sea, and as I came back I passed this place and, looking into the pool, there was the glint of the stars in the water.

"She knelt by my bed in the dark, and I could just see the glinting of her eyes as she looked at me - the stars in the shadowy waterpool!

"I had never dreamed that there could be anything so wonderful in the whole world. My father had told me of many beautiful and holy and glorious things, of all the heavenly mysteries by which those who know live for ever, all the things which the Doctor and my uncle and the other silly clergymen in the Chapel ...[1] because they don't really know anything at all about them, only their names, so they are like dogs and pigs and asses who have somehow found their way into a beautiful room, full of precious and delicate treasures. These things my father told me of long ago, of the Great Mystery of the Offering.

"And I have learned the wonders of the old venerable saints that once were marvels in our land, as the Welch poem says, and of all the great works that shone around their feet as they went upon the mountains and sought the deserts of ocean. I have seen their marks and writings cut on the edges of the rocks. I know where Sagramnus lies buried in Wlad Morgan. And I shall not forget how I saw the Blessed Cup of Teilo Agyos drawn out from golden veils on Mynydd Mawr, when the stars poured out of the jewel, and I saw the sea of the saints and the spiritual things in Cor-arbennic. My father read out to me all the histories of Teilo, Dewi, and Iltyd, of their marvellous chalices and altars of Paradise from which they made the books of the Graal afterwards; and all these things are beautiful to me. But, as the Anointed Bard said: 'With the bodily lips I receive the drink of mortal vineyards; with spiritual understanding wine from the garths of the undying. May Mihangel intercede for me that these may be mingled in one cup; let the door between body and soul be thrown open. For in that day earth will have become Paradise, and the secret sayings of the bards shall be verified.' I always knew what this meant, though my father told me that many people thought it obscure or, rather, nonsense. But it is just the same really as another poem by the same Bard, where he says:

'My sin was found out, and when the old women on the bridge pointed at me I was ashamed;
I was deeply grieved when the boys shouted rebukes as I went from Caer-Newydd.
How is it that I was not ashamed before the Finger of the Almighty?
I did not suffer agony at the rebuke of the Most High.
The fist of Rhys Fawr is more dreadful to me than the hand of God.'

"He means, I think, that our great loss is that we separate what is one and make it two; and then, having done so, we make the less real into the more real, as if we thought the glass made to hold wine more important than the wine it holds. And this is what I had felt, for it was only twice that I had known wonders in my body, when I saw the Cup of Teilo sant and when the mountains appeared in vision, and so, as the Bard says, the door is shut. The life of bodily things is hard, just as the wineglass is hard. We can touch it and feel it and see it always before us. The wine is drunk and forgotten; it cannot be held. I believe the air about us is just as substantial as a mountain or a cathedral, but unless we remind ourselves we think of the air as nothing. It is not hard. But now I was in Paradise, for body and soul were molten in one fire and went up in one flame. The mortal and the immortal vines were made one. Through the joy of the body I possessed the joy of the spirit. And it was so strange to think that all this was through a woman - through a woman I had seen dozens of times and had thought nothing of, except that she was pleasant-looking and that the colour of her hair, like copper, was very beautiful.

"I cannot understand it. I cannot feel that she is really Nelly Foran who opens the door and waits at table, for she is a miracle. How I should have wondered once if I had seen a stone by the roadside become a jewel of fire and glory! But if that were to happen, it would not be so strange as what happened to me. I cannot see now the black dress and the servant's cap and apron. I see the wonderful, beautiful body shining through the darkness of my room, the glimmering of the white flower in the dark, the stars in the forest pool.

'O gift of the everlasting!
O wonderful and hidden mystery!
Many secrets have been vouchsafed to me.
I have been long acquainted with the wisdom of the trees;
Ash and oak and elm have communicated to me from my boyhood,
The birch and the hazel and all the trees of the green wood have not been dumb.
There is a caldron rimmed with pearls of whose gifts I am not ignorant.
I will speak little of it; its treasures are known to Bards.
Many went on the search of Caer-Pedryfan,
Seven alone returned with Arthur, but my spirit was present.
Seven are the apple trees in a beautiful orchard.
I have eaten of their fruit, which is not bestowed on Saxons.
I am not ignorant of a Head which is glorious and venerable.
It made perpetual entertainment for the warriors; their joys would have been immortal.
If they had not opened the door of the south, they could have feasted for ever,
Listening to the song of the Fairy Birds of Rhiannon.
Let not anyone instruct me concerning the Glassy Isle,*

In the garments of the saints who returned from it were rich odours of Paradise.
All this I knew and yet my knowledge was ignorance,
For one day, as I walked by Caer-rhiu in the principal forest of Gwent,
I saw golden Myfanwy, as she bathed in the brook Tarógi.
Her hair flowed about her. Arthur's crown had dissolved into a shining mist.
I gazed into her blue eyes as it were into twin heavens.
All the parts of her body were adornments and miracles.
O gift of the everlasting!
O wonderful and hidden mystery!
When I embraced Myfanwy a moment became immortality! [2]

"And yet I daresay this 'golden Myfanwy' was what people call 'a common girl,' and perhaps she did rough, hard work, and nobody thought anything of her till the Bard found her bathing in the brook of Tarógi. The birds in the wood said, when they saw the nightingale: 'This is a contemptible stranger!'

"*June 24*. Since I wrote last in this book the summer has come. This morning I woke up very early, and even in this horrible place the air was pure and bright as the sun rose up and the long beams shone on the cedar outside the window. She came to me by the way they think is locked and fastened, and, just as the world is white and gold at the dawn, so was she. A blackbird began to sing beneath the window. I think it came from far, for it sang to me of morning on the mountain, and the woods all still, and a little bright brook rushing down the hillside between dark green alders, and air that must be blown from heaven.

> *There is a bird that sings in the valley of the Soar.*
> *Dewi and Tegfeth and Cybi preside over that region;*
> *Sweet is the valley, sweet the sound of its waters.*
> *There is a bird that sings in the valley of the Soar;*
> *Its voice is golden, like the ringing of the saints' bells;*
> *Sweet is the valley, echoing with melodies.*
> *There is a bird that sings in the valley of the Soar;*
> *Tegfeth in the south won red martyrdom.*
> *Her song is heard in the perpetual choirs of heaven.*
> *There is a bird that sings in the valley of the Soar;*
> *Dewi in the west had an altar from Paradise.*
> *He taught the valleys of Britain to resound with Alleluia.*
> *There is a bird that sings in the valley of the Soar;*
> *Cybi in the north was the teacher of Princes.*
> *Through him Edlogan sings praise to heaven.*
> *There is a bird that sings in the valley of the Soar*
> *When shall I hear again the notes of its melody?*
> *When shall I behold once more Gwladys in that valley?* [3]

"When I think of what I know, of the wonders of darkness and the wonders of dawn, I cannot help believing that I have found something which all the world has lost. I have heard some of the fellows talking about women. Their words and their stories are filthy, and nonsense, too. One would think that if monkeys and pigs could talk about their she-monkeys and sows, it would be just like that. I might have thought that, being only boys, they knew nothing about it, and were only making up nasty, silly tales out of their nasty, silly minds. But I have heard the poor women in the town screaming and scolding at their men, and the men swearing back; and when they think they are making love, it is the most horrible of all.

"And it is not only the boys and the poor people. There are the masters and their wives. Everybody knows that the Challises and the Redburns 'fight like cats,' as they say, and that the Head's daughter was 'put up for auction' and bought by the rich manufacturer from Birmingham - a horrible, fat beast, more than twice her age, with eyes like pig's. They called it a splendid match.

"So I began to wonder whether perhaps there are very few people in the world who know; whether the real secret is lost like the great city that was drowned in the sea and only seen by one or two. Perhaps it is more like those shining Isles that the saints sought for, where the deep apple orchards are, and all the delights of Paradise. But you had to give up everything and get into a boat without oar or sails if you wanted to find Avalon or the Glassy Isle. And sometimes the saints could stand on the rocks and see those Islands far away in the midst of the sea, and smell the sweet odours and hear the bells ringing for the feast, when other people could see and hear nothing at all.

"I often think now how strange it would be if it were found out that nearly everybody is like those who stood on the rocks and could only see the waves tossing and stretching far away, and the blue sky and the mist in the distance. I mean, if it turned out that we have all been in the wrong about everything; that we live in a world of the most wonderful treasures which we see all about us, but we don't understand, and kick the jewels into the dirt, and use the chalices for slop-pails and make the holy vestments into dish-cloths, while we worship a great beast - a monster, with the head of a monkey, the body of a pig and the hind legs of a goat, with swarming lice crawling all over it. Suppose that the people that they speak of now as 'superstitious' and 'half-savages' should turn out to be in the right, and very wise, while we are all wrong and great fools! It would be something like the man who lived in the Bright Palace. The Palace had a hundred and one doors. A hundred of them opened into gardens of delight, pleasure-houses, beautiful bowers, wonderful countries, fairy seas, caves of gold and hills of diamonds, into all the most splendid places. But one door led into a cesspool, and that was the only door that the man ever opened. It may be that his sons and his grandsons have been opening that one door ever since, till they have forgotten that there are any others, so if anyone dares to speak of the ways to the garden of delight or the hills of gold he is called a madman, or a very wicked person.

"*July 15.* The other day a very strange thing happened. I had gone for a short walk out of the town before dinner on the Dunham road and came as far as the four ways where the roads cross. It is rather pretty for Lupton just there; there is a plot of grass with a big old elm tree in the middle of it, and round the tree is a rough sort of seat, where tramps and such people are often resting. As I came along I heard some sort of music coming from the direction of the tree; it was like fairies dancing, and then there were strange solemn notes like the priests' singing, and a choir answered in a deep, rolling swell of sound, and the fairies danced again; and I thought somehow of a grey church high on the cliff above a singing sea, and the Fair People outside dancing on the close turf, while the service was going on all the while. As I came nearer I heard the sea waves and the wind and the cry of the seagulls, and again the high, wonderful chanting, as if the fairies and the rocks and the waves and the wild birds were all subject to that which was being done within the church. I wondered what it could be, and then I saw there was an old ragged man sitting on the seat under the tree, playing the fiddle all to himself, and rocking from side to side. He stopped directly he saw me, and said:

"''Ah, now, would your young honour do yourself the pleasure of giving the poor old fiddler a penny or maybe two: for Lupton is the very hell of a town altogether, and when I play to dirty rogues the Reel of the Warriors, they ask for something about Two Obadiahs - the devil's black curse be on them! And it's but dry work playing to the leaf and the green sod - the blessing of the holy saints be on your honour now, this day, and for ever! 'Tis but a scarcity of beer that I have tasted for a long day, I assure your honour.'

"I had given him a shilling because I thought his music so wonderful. He looked at me steadily as he finished talking, and his face changed. I thought he was frightened, he stared so oddly. I asked him if he was ill.

"''May I be forgiven,' he said, speaking quite gravely, without that wheedling way he had when he first spoke. 'May I be forgiven for talking so to one like yourself; for this day I have begged money from one that is to gain Red Martyrdom; and indeed that is yourself.'

"He took off his old battered hat and crossed himself, and I stared at him, I was so amazed at what he said. He picked up his fiddle, and saying 'May you remember me in the time of your glory,' he walked quickly off, going away from Lupton, and I lost sight of him at the turn of the road. I suppose he was half crazy, but he played wonderfully."

CHAPTER IV

I

The materials for the history of an odd episode in Ambrose Meyrick's life are to be found in a sort of collection he made under the title "Concerning Gaiety." The episode in question dates from about the middle of his eighteenth year.

"I do not know" - he says - "how it all happened. I had been leading two eager lives. On the outside I was playing games and going up in the school with a rush, and in the inside I was being gathered more and more into the sanctuaries of immortal things. All life was transfigured for me into a radiant glory, into a quickening and catholic sacrament; and, the fooleries of the school apart, I had more and more the sense that I was a participant in a splendid and significant ritual. I think I was beginning to be a little impatient with the outward signs: I *think* I had a feeling that it was a pity that one had to drink wine out of a cup, a pity that kernels seemed to imply shells. I wanted, in my heart, to know nothing but the wine itself flowing gloriously from vague, invisible fountains, to know the things 'that really are' in their naked beauty, without their various and elaborate draperies. I doubt whether Ruskin understood the motive of the monk who walked amidst the mountains with his eyes cast down lest he might see the depths and heights about him. Ruskin calls this a narrow asceticism; perhaps it was rather the result of a very subtle aestheticism. The monk's inner vision might be fixed with such rapture on certain invisible heights and depths, that he feared lest the sight of their visible counterparts might disturb his ecstasy. It is probable, I think, that there is a point where the ascetic principle and the aesthetic become one and the same. The Indian fakir who distorts his limbs and lies on spikes is at the one extreme, the men of the Italian Renaissance were at the other. In each case the true line is distorted and awry, for neither system attains either sanctity or beauty in the highest. The fakir dwells in *surfaces*, and the Renaissance artist dwelt in *surfaces*; in neither case is there the inexpressible radiance of the invisible world shining through the surfaces. A cup of Cellini's work is no doubt very lovely; but it is not beautiful in the same way as the old Celtic cups are beautiful.

"I think I was in some danger of going wrong at the time I am talking about. I was altogether too impatient of surfaces. Heaven forbid the notion that I was ever in danger of being in any sense of the word a Protestant; but perhaps I was rather inclined to the fundamental heresy on which Protestantism builds its objection to what is called Ritual. I suppose this heresy is really Manichee; it is a charge of corruption and evil made against the visible universe, which is affirmed to be not 'very good,' but 'very bad' - or, at all events, too bad to be used as the vehicle of spiritual truth. It is extraordinary by the way, that the thinking Protestant does not perceive that this principle damns all creeds and all Bibles and all teaching quite as effectually as it damns candles and chasubles - unless, indeed, the Protestant thinks that the logical understanding is a competent vehicle of Eternal Truth, and that God can be properly and adequately defined and explained in human speech. If he thinks that, he is an ass. Incense, vestments, candles, all ceremonies, processions, rites - all these things are miserably inadequate; but they do not abound in the horrible pitfalls, misapprehensions, errors which are inseparable from speech of men used as an expression of the Church. In a savage dance there may be a vast deal more of the truth than in many of the hymns in our hymn-books.

"After all, as Martinez said, we must even be content with what we have, whether it be censers or syllogisms, or both. The way of the censer is certainly the safer, as I have said; I suppose because the ruin of the external universe is not nearly so deep nor so virulent as the ruin of men. A flower, a piece of gold, no doubt approach their archetypes - what they were meant to be - much more nearly than man does; hence their appeal is purer than the speech or the reasoning of men.

"But in those days at Lupton my head was full of certain sentences which I had lit upon somewhere or other - I believe they must have been translations from some Eastern book. I knew about a dozen of these maxims; all I can remember now are:

> *"If you desire to be inebriated: abstain from wine."*
> *"If you desire beauty: look not on beautiful things."*
> *"If you desire to see: let your eyes be blindfolded."*
> *"If you desire love: refrain from the Beloved."*

"I expect the paradox of these sayings pleased me. One must allow that if one has the inborn appetite of the somewhat subtle, of the truth not too crudely and barely expressed, there is no such atmosphere as that of a Public School for sharpening this appetite to an edge of ravening, indiscriminate hunger. Think of our friend the Colonel, who is by way of being a *fin gourmet*; imagine him fixed in a boarding-house where the meals are a repeating cycle of Irish Stew, Boiled Rabbit, Cold Mutton and Salt Cod (without oyster or any other sause)! Then let him out and place him in the Café Anglais. With what a fierce relish would he set tooth into curious and sought-out dishes! It must be remembered that I listened every Sunday in every term to one of the Doctor's sermons, and it is really not strange that I gave an eager ear to the voice of *Persian Wisdom* - as I think the book was called. At any rate, I kept Nelly Foran at a distance for nine or ten months, and when I saw a splendid sunset I averted my eyes. I longed for a love purely spiritual, for a sunset of vision.

"I caught glimpses, too, I think, of a much more profound askesis than this. I suppose you have the *askesis* in its simplest, most rationalised form in the Case of Bill the Engine-driver - I forget in what great work of *Theologia Moralis* I found the instance; perhaps Bill was really *Quidam* in the original, and his occupation stated as that of *Nauarchus*. At all events, Bill is fond of four-ale; but he had perceived that two pots of this beverage consumed before a professional journey tended to make him rather sleepy, rather less alert, than he might be in the execution of his very responsible duties. Hence Bill, considering this, wisely contents himself with *one* pot before mounting on his cab. He has deprived himself of a sensible good in order that an equally sensible but greater good may be secured - in order that he and the passengers may run no risks on the journey. Next to this simple asceticism comes, I suppose, the ordinary discipline of the Church - the abandonment of sensible goods to secure spiritual ends, the turning away from the type to the prototype, from the sight of the eyes to the vision of the soul. For in the true asceticism, whatever its degree, there is always action to a certain end, to a perceived good. Does the self-tormenting fakir act from this motive? I don't know; but if he does not, his discipline is not asceticism at all, but folly, and impious folly, too. If he mortifies himself merely for the sake of mortifying himself; then he defiles and blasphemes the Temple. This in parenthesis.

"But, as I say, I had a very dim and distant glimpse of another region of the *askesis*. Mystics will understand me when I say that there are moments when the Dark Night of the Soul is seen to be brighter than her brightest day; there are moments when it is necessary to drive away even the angels that there may be place for the Highest. One may ascend into regions so remote from the common concerns of life that it becomes difficult to procure the help of analogy, even in the terms and processes of the Arts. But suppose a painter - I need not say that I mean an artist - who is visited by an idea so wonderful, so super-exalted in its beauty that he recognises his impotence; he knows that no pigments and no technique can do anything but grossly parody his vision. Well, he will show his greatness by *not* attempting to paint that vision: he will write on a bare canvass *vidit anima sed non pinxit manus*. And I am sure that there are many romances which have never been written. It was a highly paradoxical, even a dangerous philosophy that affirmed God to be rather *Non-Ens* than *Ens*; but there are moods in which one appreciates the thought.

"I think I caught, as I say, a distant vision of that Night which excels the Day in its splendour. It began with the eyes turned away from the sunset, with lips that refused kisses. Then there came a command to the heart to cease from longing for the dear land of Gwent, to cease from that aching desire that had never died for so many years for the sight of the old land and those hills and woods of most sweet and anguished memory. I remember once, when I was a great lout of sixteen, I went to see the Lupton Fair. I always liked the great booths and caravans and merry-go-rounds, all a blaze of barbaric green and red and gold, flaming and glowing in the middle of the trampled, sodden field against a background of Lupton and wet, grey autumn sky. There were country folk then who wore smock-frocks and looked like men in them, too. One saw scores of these brave fellows at the Fair: dull, good Jutes with flaxen hair that was almost white, and with broad pink faces. I liked to see them in the white robe and the curious embroidery; they were a note of wholesomeness, an embassage from the old English village life to our filthy 'industrial centre.' It was odd to see how they stared about them; they wondered, I think, at the beastliness of the place, and yet, poor fellows, they felt bound to admire the evidence of so much money. Yes, they were of Old England; they savoured of the long, bending, broad village street, the gable ends, the grave fronts of old mellow bricks, the thatched roofs here and there, the bulging window of the 'village shop,' the old church in decorous, somewhat dull perpendicular among the elms, and, above all, the old tavern - that excellent abode of honest mirth and honest beer, relic of the time when there were men, and men who lived. Lupton is very far removed from Hardy's land, and yet as I think of these country-folk in their smock-frocks all the essence of Hardy is distilled for me; I see the village street all white in snow, a light gleaming very rarely from an upper window, and presently, amid ringing bells, one hears the carol-singers begin:

> *Remember Adam's fall,*
> *O thou man.*

"And I love to look at the whirl of the merry-go-rounds, at the people sitting with grave enjoyment on those absurd horses as they circle round and round till one's eyes were dazed. Drums beat and thundered, strange horns blew raucous calls from all quarters, and the mechanical music to which those horses revolved belched and blazed and rattled out its everlasting monotony, checked now and again by the shriek of the steam whistle, groaning into silence for a while: then the tune clanged out once more, and the horses whirled round and round.

"But on this Fair Day of which I am speaking I left the booths and the golden, gleaming merry-go-rounds for the next field, where horses were excited to brief madness and short energy. I had scarcely taken up my stand when a man close by me raised his voice to a genial shout as he saw a friend a little way off. And he spoke with the beloved accent of Gwent, with those tones that come to me more ravishing, more enchanting than all the music in the world. I had not heard them for years of weary exile! Just a phrase or two of common greeting in those chanting accents: the Fair passed away, was whirled into nothingness, its shouting voices, the charging of horses, drum and trumpet, clanging, metallic music - it rushed down into the abyss. There was the silence that follows a great peal of thunder; it was early morning and I was standing in a well-remembered valley, beside the blossoming thorn bush, looking far away to the wooded hills that kept the East, above the course of the shining river. I was, I say, a great lout of sixteen, but the tears flooded my eyes, my heart swelled with its longing.

"Now, it seemed, I was to quell such thoughts as these, to desire no more the fervent sunlight on the mountain, or the sweet scent of the dusk about the runnings of the brook. I had been very fond of 'going for walks' - walks of the imagination. I was afraid, I suppose, that unless by constant meditation I renewed the shape of the old land in my mind, its image might become a blurred and fading picture; I should forget little by little the ways of those deep, winding lanes that took courses that were almost subterranean over hill and vale, by woodside and waterside, narrow, cavernous, leaf-vaulted; cool in the greatest heats of summer. And the wandering paths that crossed the fields, that led one down into places hidden and remote, into still depths where no one save myself ever seemed to enter, that sometimes ended with a certain solemnity at a broken stile in a hedgerow grown into a thicket - within a plum tree returning to the savage life of the wood, a forest, perhaps, of blue lupins, and a great wild rose about the ruined walls of a house - all these ways I must keep in mind as if they were mysteries and great secrets, as indeed they were. So I strolled in memory through the Pageant of Gwent: 'lest I should forget the region of the flowers, lest I should become unmindful of the wells and the floods.'

"But the time came, as I say, when it was represented to me that all this was an indulgence which, for a season at least, must be pretermitted. With an effort I voided my soul of memory and desire and weeping; when the idols of doomed Twyn-Barlwm, and great Mynydd Maen, and the silver esses of the Usk appeared before me, I cast them out; I would not meditate white Caerleon shining across the river. I endured, I think, the severest pains. De Quincey, that admirable artist, that searcher into secrets and master of mysteries, has described my pains for me under the figure of the Opium Eater breaking the bonds of his vice. How often, when the abominations of Lupton, its sham energies, its sham morals, its sham enthusiasms, all its battalia of cant surged and beat upon me, have I been sorely tempted to yield, to suffer no more the press of folly, but to steal away by a secret path I knew, to dwell in a secure valley where the foolish could never trouble me. Sometimes I 'fell,' as I drank deep then of the magic well-water, and went astray in the green dells and avenues of the wildwood. Still I struggled to refrain my heart from these things, to keep my spirit under the severe discipline of abstention; and with a constant effort I succeeded more and more.

"But there was a yet deeper depth in this process of *catharsis*. I have said that sometimes one must expel the angels that God may have room; and now the strict ordinance was given that I should sever myself from that great dream of Celtic sanctity that for me had always been *the* dream, the innermost shrine in which I could take refuge, the house of sovran medicaments where all the wounds of soul and body were healed. One does not wish to be harsh; we must admit, I suppose, that moderate, sensible Anglicanism must have *something* in it - since the absolute sham cannot very well continue to exist. Let us say, then, that it is highly favourable to a respectable and moral life, that it encourages a temperate and well-regulated spirit of devotion. It was certainly a very excellent and (according to her lights) devout woman who, in her version of the *Anima Christi* altered 'inebriate me' to 'purify me,' and it was a good cleric who hated the Vulgate reading, *calix meus inebrians*. My father had always instructed me that we must conform outwardly, and bear with *Dearly Beloved Brethren*; while we celebrated in our hearts the Ancient Mass of the Britons, and waited for Cadwaladr to return. I reverenced his teaching, I still reverence it, and agree that we must conform; but in my heart I have always doubted whether moderate Anglicanism be Christianity in any sense, whether it even deserves to be called a religion at all. I do not doubt, of course, that many truly religious people have professed it: I speak of the system, and of the atmosphere which emanates from it. And when the Public School *ethos* is added to this - well, the resultant teaching comes pretty much to the dogma that Heaven and the Head are strict allies. One must not degenerate into ecclesiastical controversy; I merely want to say that I never dreamed of looking for religion in our Chapel services. No doubt the *Te Deum* was still the *Te Deum*, but the noblest of hymns is degraded, obscured, defiled, made ridiculous, if you marry it to a tune that would disgrace a penny gaff. Personally, I think that the airs on the piano-organs are much more reverend compositions than Anglican chants, and I am sure that many popular hymn tunes are vastly inferior in solemnity to *'E Dunno where 'e are*.

"No; the religion that led me and drew me and compelled me was that wonderful and doubtful mythos of the Celtic Church. It was the study - nay, more than the study, the enthusiasm - of my father's life; and as I was literally baptized with water from a Holy Well, so spiritually the great legend of the Saints and their amazing lives had tinged all my dearest aspirations, had become to me the glowing vestment of the Great Mystery. One may sometimes be deeply interested in the matter of a tale while one is wearied or sickened by the manner of it; one may have to embrace the bright divinity on the horrid lips of the serpent of Cos. Or, on the other hand, the manner - the style - may be admirable, and the matter a mere nothing but a ground for the embroidery. But for me the Celtic Mythos was the Perfect Thing, the King's Daughter: *Omnis gloria ejus filiæ Regis ab, intus, in fimbriis aureis circumamicta varietatibus*. I have learned much more of this great mystery since those days - I have seen, that is, how entirely, how absolutely my boyhood's faith was justified; but even then with but little knowledge I was rapt at the thought of this marvellous knight-errantry, of this Christianity which was not a moral code, with some sort of metaphorical Heaven held out as a reward for its due observance, but a great mystical adventure into the unknown sanctity. Imagine a Bishop of the Established Church getting into a boat without oar or sails! Imagine him, if you can, doing anything remotely analogous to such an action. Conceive the late Archbishop Tait going apart into the chapel at Lambeth for three days and three nights; then you may well conceive the people in the opposite bank being dazzled with the blinding supernatural light poured forth from the chapel windows. Of course, the end of the Celtic Church was ruin and confusion - but Don Quixote failed and fell, while Sancho Panza lived a fat, prosperous peasant. He inherited, I think, a considerable sum from the knight, and was, no doubt, a good deal looked up to in the village.

"Yes; the Celtic Church was the Company of the Great Errantry, of the Great Mystery, and, though all the history of it seems but a dim and shadowy splendour, its burning rose-red lamp yet glows for a few, and from my earliest childhood I was indoctrinated in the great Rite of Cor-arbennic. When I was still very young I had been humoured with the sight of a wonderful Relic of the Saints - never shall I forget that experience of the holy magic of sanctity. Every little wood, every rock and fountain, and every running stream of Gwent were hallowed for me by some mystical and entrancing legend, and the thought of this High Spiritual City and its Blessed Congregation could, in a moment, exercise and drive forth from me all the ugly and foolish and gibbering spectres that made up the life of that ugly and foolish place where I was imprisoned.

"Now, with a sorrowful farewell, I bade good-bye for a brief time (as I hoped it would be) to this golden legend; my heart was emptied of its treasures and its curious shows, and the lights on the altars were put out, and the images were strictly veiled. Hushed was the chanting in the Sovereign and Perpetual Choir, hidden were the High Hallows of the Saints, no more did I follow them to their cells in the wild hills, no more did I look from the rocks in the west and see them set forth for Avalon. Alas!

"A great silence seemed to fall upon me, the silence of the depths beneath the earth. And with the silence there was darkness. Only in a hidden place there was reserved the one taper - the Light of Conformity, of a perfect submission, that from the very excess of sorrow and deprivation drew its secret but quintessential joy. I am reminded, now that I look back upon this great purgation of the soul, of the story that I once read of the Arabic Alchemist. He came to the Caliph Haroun with a strange and extravagant proposal. Haroun sat in all his splendour, his viziers, his chamberlains, his great officers about him, in his golden court which displayed all the wonders and superfluities of the East. He gave judgment; the wicked were punished, the virtuous were rewarded; God's name was exalted, the Prophet was venerated. There came before the Commander of the Faithful a poor old man in the poor and ragged robes of a wandering poet; he was oppressed by the weight of his years, and his entrance was like the entrance of misery. So wretched was his appearance that one of the chamberlains, who was well acquainted with the poets, could not help quoting the well-known verses:

"'Between the main and a drop of rain the difference seen is nothing great.
The sun so bright and the taper's light are alike and one save in pomp and state.
In the grain of sand and in all the land what may ye arraign as disparate?
A crust of bread and a King's board spread will hunger's lust alike abate.
With the smallest blade or with host arrayed the Ruler may quench his gall and hate.
A stone in a box and a quarry of rocks may be shown to be of an equal freight.
With a sentence bold or with gold untold the lover may hold or capture his mate.
The King and the Bard may alike be debarred from the fold of the Lord
Compassionate.'"

"The Commander of the Faithful praised God, the Merciful, the Compassionate, the King of the Day of Judgment, and caused the chamberlain to be handsomely rewarded. He then enquired of the old man for what reason he came before him, and the beggar (as, indeed, he seemed) informed the Caliph that he had for many years prosecuted his studies in magic, alchemy, astrology and geomancy and all other curious and surprising arts, in Spain, Grand Cairo, the land of the Moors, India, China, in various Cities of the Infidels; in fact, in every quarter of the world where magicians were to be found. In proof of his proficiency he produced a little box which he carried about him for the purpose of his geomantic operations and asked anyone who was willing to stand forth, that he might hear his whole life, past, present and future. The Caliph ordered one of his officers to submit himself to this ordeal, and the beggar having made the points in the sand, and having erected the figure according to the rules of the geomantic art, immediately informed the officer of all the most hidden transactions in which he had been engaged, including several matters which this officer thought had been secrets locked in his own breast. He also foretold his death in a year's time from a certain herb, and so it fell out, for he was strangled with a hempen cord by order of the Caliph. In the meantime, the Commander of the Faithful and all about him were astonished, and the Beggar Magician was ordered to proceed with his story. He spoke at great length, and everyone remarked the elegance and propriety of his diction, which was wanting in no refinement of classical eloquence. But the sum of his speech was this - that he had discovered the greatest wonder of the whole world, the name of which he declared was Asrar, and by this talisman he said that the Caliph might make himself more renowned than all the kings that had ever reigned on the earth, not excepting King Solomon, the son of David. This was the method of the operation which the beggar proposed. The Commander of the Faithful was to gather together all the wealth of his entire kingdom, omitting nothing that could possibly be discovered; and while this was being done the magician said that he would construct a furnace of peculiar shape in which all these splendours and magnificences and treasures of the world must be consumed in a certain fire of art, prepared with wisdom. And at last, he continued, after the operation had endured many days, the fire being all the while most curiously governed, there would remain but one drop no larger than a pearl, but glorious as the sun to the moon and all the starry heavens and the wonders of the compassionate; and with this drop the Caliph Haroun might heal all the sorrows of the universe. Both the Commander of the Faithful and all his viziers and officers were stupefied by this proposal, and most of the assemblage considered the beggar to be a madman. The Caliph, however, asked him to return the next day in order that his plans might receive more mature consideration.

"The beggar prostrated himself and went forth from the hall of audience, but he returned no more, nor could it be discovered that he had been seen again by anyone.

"'But one drop no larger than a pearl,' and 'where there is Nothing there is All.' I have often thought of those sentences in looking back on that time when, as Chesson said, I was one of those 'light-hearted and yet sturdy and reliable young fellows to whose hands the honour and safety of England might one day be committed.' I cast all the treasures I possessed into the alembic; again and again they were rectified by the heat of the fire 'most curiously governed'; I saw the 'engendering of the Crow' black as pitch, the flight of the Dove with Silver Wings, and at last Sol rose red and glorious, and I fell down and gave thanks to heaven for this most wonderful gift, the 'Sun blessed of the Fire.' I had dispossessed myself of all, and I found that I possessed all; I had thrown away all the money in my purse, and I was richer than I had ever been; I had died, and I had found a new life in the land of the living.

"It is curious that I should now have to explain the pertinency of all that I have written to the title of this Note - concerning Gaiety. It should not be necessary. The chain of thought is almost painfully obvious. But I am afraid it is necessary.

"Well: I once read an interesting article in the daily paper. It was written apropos of some Shakespearean celebrations or other, and its purport was that modern England was ever so much happier than mediæval or Elizabethan England. It is possible that an acute logician might find something to say on this thesis; but my interest lay in the following passages, which I quote:

"'Merrie England,' with its maypoles and its Whitsun Ales, and its Shrove-tide jousts and junketings is dead for us, from the religious point of view. The England that has survived is, after all, a greater England still. It is Puritan England.... The spirit has gone. Surely it is useless to revive the form. Wherefore should the May Queen be "holy, wise, and fair," if not to symbolise the Virgin Mary? And as for Shrove-tide, too, what point in jollity without a fast to follow?'

"The article is not over-illuminating, but I think the writer had caught a glimpse of the truth that there is a deep relation between Mirth and Sanctity; that no real mirth is possible without the apprehension of the mysteries as its antecedent. The fast and the feast are complementary terms. He is right; there is no point in jollity unless there is a fast or something of the nature of a fast to follow - though, of course, there is nothing to hinder the most advanced thinker from drinking as much fusel-oil and raw Russian spirit as he likes. But the result of this course is not real mirth or jollity; it is perhaps more essentially dismal than a 'Tea' amongst the Protestant Dissenters. And, on the other hand, true gaiety is only possible to those who have fasted; and now perhaps it will be seen that I have been describing the preparations for a light-hearted festival.

"The cloud passed away from me, the restrictions and inhibitions were suddenly removed, and I woke up one morning in dancing, bubbling spirits, every drop of blood in my body racing with new life, my nerves tingling and thrilling with energy. I laughed as I awoke; I was conscious that I was to engage in a strange and fantastic adventure, though I had not the remotest notion of what it was to be."

II

Ambrose Meyrick's adventure was certainly of the fantastic order. His fame had long been established on a sure footing with his uncle and with everybody else, and Mr. Horbury had congratulated him with genuine enthusiasm on his work in the examinations - the Summer term was drawing to a close. Mr. Horbury was Ambrose's trustee, and he made no difficulty about signing a really handsome cheque for his nephew's holiday expenses and outfit. "There," he said "you ought to be able to do pretty well on that. Where do you think of going?"

Ambrose said that he had thought of North Devon, of tramping over Exmoor, visiting the Doone country, and perhaps of working down to Dartmoor.

"You couldn't do better. You ought to try your hand at fishing: wonderful sport in some of those streams. It mightn't come off at first, but with your eye and sense of distance you'll soon make a fine angler. If you *do* have a turn at the trout, get hold of some local man and make him give you a wrinkle or two. It's no good getting your flies from town. Now, when I was fishing in Hampshire - - "

Mr. Horbury went on; but the devil of gaiety had already dictated a wonderful scheme to Ambrose, and that night he informed Nelly Foran that she must alter her plans; she was to come with him to France instead of spending a fortnight at Blackpool. He carried out this mad device with an ingenuity that poor Mr. Palmer would certainly have called "diabolical." In the first place, there was to be a week in London - for Nelly must have some clothes; and this week began as an experience of high delight. It was not devoid of terror, for masters might be abroad, and Ambrose did not wish to leave Lupton for some time. However, they neither saw nor were seen. Arriving at St. Pancras, the luggage was left in the station, and Ambrose, who had studied the map of London, stood for a while on the pavement outside Scott's great masterpiece of architecture and considered the situation with grave yet humorous deliberation. Nelly proved herself admirably worthy of the adventure; its monstrous audacity appealed to her, and she was in a state of perpetual subdued laughter for some days after their arrival. Meyrick looked about him and found that the Euston Road, being squalid and noisy, offered few attractions; and with sudden resolution he took the girl by the arm and steered into the heart of Bloomsbury. In this charmingly central and yet retired quarter they found rooms in a quiet byway which, oddly enough, looked on a green field; and under the pleasant style of Mr. and Mr. Lupton they partook of tea while the luggage was fetched by somebody - probably a husband - who came with a shock of red, untidy hair from the dark bowels of the basement. They screamed with mirth over the meal. Mr. Horbury had faults, but he kept a good table for himself, his boys and his servants; and the exotic, quaint flavour of the "bread" and "butter" seemed to these two young idiots exquisitely funny. And the queer, faint, close smell, too, of the whole house - it rushed out at one when the hall door was opened: it was heavy, and worth its weight in gold.

"I never know," Ambrose used to say afterwards, "whether to laugh or cry when I have been away for some time from town, and come back and smell that wonderful old London aroma. I don't believe it's so strong or so rare as it used to be; I have been disappointed once or twice in houses in quite shabby streets. It was *there*, of course, but - well, if it were a vintage wine I should say it was a second growth of a very poor year - Margaux, no doubt, but a Margaux of one of those very indifferent years in the early 'seventies. Or it may be like the smell of grease-paints; one doesn't notice it after a month or two. But I don't think it is.

"Still," he would go on, "I value what I can smell of it. It brings back to me that afternoon, that hot, choking afternoon of ever so many years ago. It was really tremendously hot - ninety-two degrees, I think I saw in the paper the next day - and when we got out at St. Pancras the wind came at one like a furnace blast. There was no sun visible; the sky was bleary - a sort of sickly, smoky yellow, and the burning wind came in gusts, and the dust hissed and rattled on the pavement. Do you know what a low public-house smells like in London on a hot afternoon? Do you know what London bitter tastes like on such a day - the publican being evidently careful of his clients' health, and aware of the folly of drinking cold beverages during a period of extreme heat? I do. Nelly, poor dear, had warm lemonade, and I had warm beer - warm chemicals, I mean. But the odour! Why doesn't some scientific man stop wasting his time over a lot of useless rubbish and discover a way of bottling the odour of the past?

"Ah! but if he did so, in a phial of rare crystal with a stopper as secure as the seal of Solimaun ben Daoud would I preserve one most precious scent, inscribing on the seal, within a perfect pentagram, the mystic legend 'No. 15, Little Russell Row.'"

The cat had come in with the tea-tray. He was a black cat, not very large, with a decent roundness of feature, and yet with a suggestion of sinewy skinniness about him - the Skinniness of the wastrel, not of the poor starveling. His bright green eyes had, as Ambrose observed, the wisdom of Egypt; on his tomb should be inscribed "The Justified in Sekht." He walked solemnly in front of the landlady, his body describing strange curves, his tail waving in the air, and his ears put back with an expression of intense cunning. He seemed delighted at "the let," and when Nelly stroked his back he gave a loud shriek of joy and made known his willingness to take a little refreshment.

They laughed so heartily over their tea that when the landlady came in to clear the things away they were still bubbling over with aimless merriment.

"I likes to see young people 'appy," she said pleasantly, and readily provided a latchkey in case they cared to come in rather late. She told them a good deal of her life: she had kept lodgings in Judd Street, near King's Cross - a nasty, noisy street, she called it - and she seemed to think the inhabitants a low lot. She had to do with all sorts, some good some bad, and the business wasn't what it had been in her mother's day.

They sat a little while on the sofa, hand in hand still consumed with the jest of their being there at all, and imagining grotesque entrances of Mr. Horbury or Dr. Chesson. Then they went out to wander about the streets, to see London easily, merrily, without bothering the Monument, or the British Museum, or Madame Tussaud's - finally, to get something to eat, they didn't know when or where or how, and they didn't in the least care! There was one "sight" they were not successful in avoiding: they had not journeyed far before the great portal of the British Museum confronted them, grandiose and gloomy. So, by the sober way of Great Russell Street, they made their way into Tottenham Court Road and, finally, into Oxford Street. The shops were bright and splendid, the pavement was crowded with a hurrying multitude, as it seemed to the country folk, though it was the dullest season of the year. It was a great impression - decidedly London was a wonderful place. Already Ambrose felt a curious sense of being at home in it; it was not beautiful, but it was on the immense scale; it did something more than vomit stinks into the air, poison into the water and rows of workmen's houses on the land. They wandered on, and then they had the fancy that they would like to explore the regions to the south; it was so impossible, as Ambrose said, to know where they would find themselves eventually. He carefully lost himself within a few minutes of Oxford Street. A few turnings to right and then to left; the navigation of strange alleys soon left them in the most satisfactory condition of bewilderment; the distinctions of the mariner's compass, its pedantry of east and west, north and south, were annihilated and had ceased to be; it was an adventure in a trackless desert, in the Australian bush, but on safer ground and in an infinitely more entertaining scene. At first they had passed through dark streets, Georgian and Augustan ways, gloomy enough, and half deserted; there were grave houses, with many stories of windows, now reduced to printing offices, to pickle warehouses, to odd crafts such as those of the metal assayer, the crucible maker, the engraver of seals, the fabricator of Boule. But how wonderful it was to see the actual place where those things were done! Ambrose had read of such arts, but had always thought of them as existing in a vague void - if some of them even existed at all in those days: but there in the windows were actual crucibles, strange-looking curvilinear pots of grey-yellowish ware, the veritable instruments of the Magnum Opus, inventions of Arabia. He was no longer astonished when a little farther he saw a harpsichord, which had only been a name to him, a beautiful looking thing, richly inlaid, with its date - 1780 - inscribed on a card above it. It was now utterly wonderland: he could very likely buy armour round the corner; and he had scarcely formed the thought when a very fine sixteenth-century suit, richly damascened, rose up before him, handsomely displayed between two black jacks. These were the comparatively silent streets; but they turned a corner, and what a change! All the roadway, not the pavement only, seemed full of a strolling, chatting, laughing mob of people: the women were bareheaded, and one heard nothing but the roll of the French "r," torrents of sonorous sound trolled out with the music of happy song. The papers in the shops were all French, ensigns on every side proclaimed "Vins Fins," "Beaune Supérieur": the tobacconists kept their tobacco in square blue, yellow and brown packets; "Charcuterie" made a brave and appetising show. And here was a "Café Restaurant: au château de Chinon." The name was enough; they could not dine elsewhere, and Ambrose felt that he was honouring the memory of the great Rabelais.

It was probably not a very good dinner. It was infinitely better than the Soho dinner of these days, for the Quarter had hardly begun to yield to the attack of Art, Intellect and the Suburbs which, between them, have since destroyed the character and unction of many a good cook-shop. Ambrose only remembered two dishes; the pieds de porc grillés and the salad. The former he thought both amusing and delicious, and the latter was strangely and artfully compounded of many herbs, of little vinegar, of abundant Provençal oil, with the *chapon*, or crust rubbed with garlic, reposing at the bottom of the bowl after Madame had "tormented" the ingredients - the salad was a dish from Fairyland. There be no such salads now in all the land of Soho.

"Let me celebrate, above all, the little red wine," says Ambrose in a brief dithyrambic note. "Not in any mortal vineyard did its father grape ripen; it was not nourished by the warmth of the visible sun, nor were the rains that made it swell common waters from the skies above us. Not even in the Chinonnais, sacred earth though that be, was the press made that caused its juices to be poured into the *cuve*, nor was the humming of its fermentation heard in any of the good cellars of the lower Touraine. But in that region which Keats celebrates when he sings the 'Mermaid Tavern' was this juice engendered - the vineyard lay low down in the south, among the starry plains where is the *Terra Turonensis Celestis*, that unimaginable country which Rabelais beheld in his vision where mighty Gargantua drinks from inexhaustible vats eternally, where Pantagruel is athirst for evermore, though he be satisfied continually. There, in the land of the Crowned Immortal Tosspots was that wine of ours vintaged, red with the rays of the Dog-star, made magical by the influence of Venus, fertilised by the happy aspect of Mercury. O rare, superabundant and most excellent juice, fruit of all fortunate stars, by thee were we translated, exalted into the fellowship of that Tavern of which the old poet writes: *Mihi est propositum in Taberna mori!*"

There were few English people in the Château de Chinon - indeed, it is doubtful whether there was more than one - the ménage Lupton excepted. This one compatriot happened to be a rather remarkable man - it was Carrol. He was not in the vanguard of anything; he knew no journalists and belonged to no clubs; he was not even acquainted in the most distant manner with a single person who could be called really influential or successful. He was an obscure literary worker, who published an odd volume every five or six years: now and then he got notices, when there was no press of important stuff in the offices, and sometimes a kindly reviewer predicted that he would come out all right in time, though he had still much to learn. About a year before he died, an intelligent reading public was told that one or two things of his were rather good; then, on his death, it was definitely discovered that the five volumes of verse occupied absolutely unique ground, that a supreme poet had been taken from us, a poet who had raised the English language into a fourth dimension of melody and magic. The intelligent reading public read him no more than they ever did, but they buy him in edition after edition, from large quarto to post octavo; they buy him put up into little decorated boxes; they buy him on Japanese vellum; they buy him illustrated by six different artists; they discuss no end of articles about him; they write their names in the Carrol Birthday Book; they set up the Carrol Calendar in their boudoirs; they have quotations from him in Westminster Abbey and St. Paul's Cathedral; they sing him in the famous Carrol Cycle of Song; and, last and best of all, a brilliant American playwright is talking even now of dramatising him. The Carrol Club, of course, is ancient history. Its membership is confined to the ranks of intellect and art; it invites to its dinners foreign princes, bankers, major-generals and other persons of distinction - all of whom, of course, are intensely interested in the master's book; and the record and praise of the Club are in all the papers. It is a pity that Carrol is dead. He would not have sworn: he would have grinned.

Even then, though he was not glorious, he was observant, and he left a brief note, a sort of thumb-nail sketch, of his impressions that night at the Château de Chinon.

"I was sitting in my old corner," he says, "wondering why the devil I wrote so badly on the whole, and what the devil I was going to do with the subject that I had tackled. The dinner was not so bad at the old Château in those days, though now they say the plate-glass is the best dish in the establishment. I liked the old place; it was dingy and low down and rather disreputable, I fancy, and the company was miscellaneous French with a dash of Italian. Nearly all of us knew each other, and there were regulars who sat in the same seat night after night. I liked it all. I liked the coarse tablecloths and the black-handled knives and the lead spoons and the damp, adhesive salt, and the coarse, strong, black pepper that one helped with a fork handle. Then there was Madame sitting on high, and I never saw an uglier woman nor a more good-natured. I was getting through my roast fowl and salad that evening, when two wonderful people came in, obviously from fairyland! I saw they had never been in such a place in all their lives before - I don't believe either of them had set foot in London until that day, and their wonder and delight and enjoyment of it all were so enormous that I had another helping of food and an extra half-bottle of wine. I enjoyed them, too, in their way, but I could see that their fowl and their wine were not a bit the same as mine. I once knew the restaurant they were really dining at - Grand Café de Paradis - some such name as that. He was an extraordinary looking chap, quite young, I should fancy, black hair, dark skin, and such burning eyes! I don't know why, but I felt he was a bit out of his setting, and I kept thinking how I should like to see him in a monk's robe. Madame was different. She was a lovely girl with amazing copper hair; dressed rather badly - of the people, I should imagine. But what a gaiety she had! I couldn't hear what they were saying, but one had to smile with sheer joy at the sight of her face - it positively danced with mirth, and a good musician could have set it to music, I am sure. There was something a little queer - too pronounced, perhaps - about the lower part of her face. Perhaps it would have been an odd tune, but I know I should have liked to hear it!"

Ambrose lit a black Caporal cigarette - he had bought a packet on his way. He saw an enticing bottle, of rotund form, paying its visits to some neighbouring tables, and the happy fools made the acquaintance of Benedictine.

"Oh, yes, it is all very well," Ambrose has been heard to say on being offered this agreeable and aromatic liqueur, "it's nice enough, I daresay. But you should have tasted the *real* stuff. I got it at a little cafe in Soho some years ago - the Château de Chinon. No, it's no good going there now, it's quite different. All the walls are plate-glass and gold; the head waiter is called Maître d'hôtel, and I am told it's quite the thing, both in southern and northern suburbs, to make up dinner parties at the Château - everything most correct, evening dress, fans, opera cloaks, 'Hide-seek' champagne, and stalls afterwards. One gets a glimpse of Bohemian life that way, and everybody says it's been such a queer evening, but quite amusing, too. But you can't get the real Benedictine there now.

"Where can you get it? Ah! I wish I knew. I never come across it. The bottle looks just the same, but it's quite a different flavour. The phylloxera may be responsible, of course, but I don't think it is. Perhaps the bottle that went round the table that night was like the powder in *Jekyll and Hyde* - its properties were the result of some strange accident. At all events, they were quite magical."

The two adventurers went forth into the maze of streets and lost themselves again. Heaven knows where they went, by what ways they wandered, as with wide-gleaming eyes, arm locked in arm, they gazed on an enchanted scene which they knew must be London and nothing else - what else could it be? Indeed, now and again, Ambrose thought he recognized certain features and monuments and public places of which he had read; but still! That wine of the Château was, by all mundane reckonings, of the smallest, and one little glass of Benedictine with coffee could not disturb the weakest head: yet was it London, after all?

What they saw was, doubtless, the common world of the streets and squares, the gay ways and the dull, the broad, ringing, lighted roads and the dark, echoing passages; yet they saw it all as one sees a mystery play, through a veil. But the veil before their eyes was a transmuting vision, and its substance was shot as if it were samite, with wonderful and admirable golden ornaments. In the Eastern Tales, people find themselves thus suddenly transported into an unknown magical territory, with cities that are altogether things of marvel and enchantment, whose walls are pure gold, lighted by the shining of incomparable jewels; and Ambrose declared later that never till that evening had he realized the extraordinary and absolute truth to nature of the *Arabian Nights*. Those who were present on a certain occasion will not soon forget his rejoinder to "a gentleman in the company" who said that for truth to nature he went to George Eliot.

"I was speaking of men and women, Sir," was the answer, "not of lice."

The gentleman in question, who was quite an influential man - some whisper that he was an editor - was naturally very much annoyed.

Still, Ambrose maintained his position. He would even affirm that for crude realism the Eastern Tales were absolutely unique.

"Of course," he said, "I take realism to mean absolute and essential truthfulness of description, as opposed to merely conventional treatment. Zola is a realist, not - as the imbeciles suppose - because he described - well, rather minutely - many unpleasant sights and sounds and smells and emotions, but because he was a poet, a seer; because, in spite of his pseudo-philosophies, his cheap materialisms, he saw the true heart, the reality of things. Take *La Terre*; do you think it is 'realistic' because it describes minutely, and probably faithfully, the event of a cow calving? Not in the least; the local vet. who was called in could probably do all that as well, or better. It is 'realist' because it goes behind all the brutalities, all the piggeries and inhumanities, of those frightful people, and shows us the strange, mad, transcendent passion that lay behind all those things - the wild desire for the land - a longing that burned, that devoured, that inflamed, that drove men to hell and death as would a passion for a goddess who might never be attained. Remember how 'La Beauce' is personified, how the earth swells and quickens before one, how every clod and morsel of the soil cries for its service and its sacrifice and its victims - I call *that* realism.

"The *Arabian Nights* is also profoundly realistic, though both the subject-matter and the method of treatment - the technique - are very different from the subject-matter and the technique of Zola. Of course, there may be people who think that if you describe a pigsty well you are a 'realist,' and if you describe an altar well you are 'romantic.' ... I do not know that the mental processes of Crétins form a very interesting subject for discussion."

One may surmise, if one will, that the sudden violence of the change was a sufficient cause of exaltation. That detestable Lupton left behind; no town, but a collection of stink and poison factories and slave quarters; that more detestable school, more ridiculous than the Academy of Lagado; that most detestable routine, games, lessons and the Doctor's sermons - the transition was tremendous to the freedom of fabled London, of the unknown streets and unending multitudes.

Ambrose said he hesitated to talk of that walk, lest he should be thought an aimless liar. They strolled for hours seeing the most wonderful things, the most wonderful people; but he declared that the case was similar to that of the Benedictine - he could never discover again the regions that he had perambulated. Somewhere, he said, close to the Château de Chinon there must be a passage which had since been blocked up. By it was the entrance to Fairyland.

When at last they found Little Russell Row, the black cat was awaiting them with an expression which was pleased and pious, too; he had devoured the greater portion of that quarter-pound of dubious butter. Ambrose smoked black cigarettes in bed till the packet was finished.

III

It was an amazing week they spent in London. For a couple of days Nelly was busied in getting "things" and "odds and ends," and, to her credit, she dressed the part most admirably. She abjured all the imperial purples, the Mediterranean blues, the shrieking lilacs that her class usually affects, and appeared at last a model of neat gaiety.

In the meantime, while these shopping expeditions were in progress, while Nelly consulted with those tall, dark-robed, golden-haired and awful Elegances which preside over the last mysteries of the draper and milliner, Ambrose sat at home in Little Russell Row and worked out the outlines of some fantasies that had risen in his mind. It was, in fact, during these days that he made the notes which were afterwards expanded into the curious *Defence of Taverns*, a book which is now rare and sought after by collectors. It is supposed that it was this work that was in poor Palmer's mind when the earnest man referred with a sort of gloomy reticence to Meyrick's later career. He had, in all probability, not read a line of it; but the title was certainly not a very pleasing one, judged by ordinary scholastic standards. And it must be said that the critical reception of the book was not exactly encouraging. One paper wondered candidly why such a book was ever written or printed; another denounced the author in good, set terms as an enemy of the great temperance movement; while a third, a Monthly Reviewer, declared that the work made his blood boil. Yet even the severest moralists should have seen by the epigraph that the Apes and Owls and Antiques hid mysteries of some sort, since a writer whose purposes were really evil and intemperate would never have chosen such a motto as: *Jalalúd-Din praised the behaviour of the Inebriated and drank water from the well.* But the reviewers thought that this was unintelligible nonsense, and merely a small part of the writer's general purpose to annoy.

The rough sketch is contained in the first of the *Note Books*, which are still unpublished, and perhaps are likely to remain so. Meyrick jotted down his hints and ideas in the dingy "first floor front" of the Bloomsbury lodging-house, sitting at the rosewood "Davenport" which, to the landlady, seemed the last word in beautiful furniture.

The ménage rose late. What a relief it was to be free of the horrible bells that poisoned one's rest at Lupton, to lie in peace as long as one liked, smoking a matutinal cigarette or two to the accompaniment of a cup of tea! Nelly was acquiring the art of the cigarette-smoker by degrees. She did not like the taste at all at first, but the wild and daring deviltry of the practice sustained her, and she persevered. And while they thus wasted the best hours of the day, Ambrose would make to pass before the bottom of the bed a long procession of the masters, each uttering his characteristic word of horror and astonishment as he went by, each whirled away by some invisible power in the middle of a sentence. Thus would enter Chesson, fully attired in cassock, cap and gown:

"Meyrick! It is impossible? Are you not aware that such conduct as this is entirely inconsistent with the tone of a great Public School? Have the Games ..." But he was gone; his legs were seen vanishing in a whirlwind which bore him up the chimney.

Then Horbury rose out of the carpet:

"Plain living and clear thinking are the notes of the System. A Spartan Discipline - Meyrick! Do you call this a Spartan Discipline? Smoking tobacco and reposing with ..." He shot like an arrow after the Head.

"We discourage luxury by every means in our power. Boy! This is luxury! Boy, boy! You are like the later Romans, boy! Heliogabalus was accustomed ..." The chimney consumed Palmer also; and he gave place to another.

"Roughly speaking, a boy should be always either in school or playing games. He should never be suffered to be at a loose end. Is this your idea of playing games? I tell you, Meyrick ..."

The game amused Nelly, more from its accompanying "business" and facial expression than from any particular comprehension of the dialogue. Ambrose saw that she could not grasp all the comedy of his situations, so he invented an Idyll between the Doctor and a notorious and flamboyant barmaid at the "Bell." The fame of this lady ran great but not gracious through all Lupton. This proved a huge success; beginning as a mere episode, it gathered to itself a complicated network of incidents and adventures, of wild attempts and strange escapes, of stratagems and ambushes, of disguises and alarms. Indeed, as Ambrose instructed Nelly with great solemnity, the tale, at first an idyll, the simple, pastoral story of the loves of the Shepherd Chesson and the Nymph Bella, was rapidly becoming epical in its character. He talked of dividing it into twelve books! He enlarged very elaborately the Defeat of the Suitors. In this the dear old Head, disguised as a bookmaker, drugged the whisky of the young bloods who were accustomed to throng about the inner bar of the "Bell." There was quite a long passage describing the compounding of the patent draught from various herbs, the enormous cook at the Head's house enacting a kind of Canidia part, and helping in the concoction of the dose.

"Mrs. Belper," the Doctor would observe, "This is *most* gratifying. I had no idea that your knowledge of simples was so extensive. Do I understand you to affirm that those few leaves which you hold in your hand will produce marked symptoms?"

"Bless your dear 'art, Doctor Chesson, and if you'll forgive me for talking so to such a learned gentleman, and so good, I'm sure, but you'll find there's nothing in the world like it. Often and often have I 'eard my pore old mother that's dead and gone these forty year come Candlemas ..."

"Mrs. Belper, Mrs. Belper, I am surprised at you! Are you not aware that the Judicial Committee of the Privy Council has pronounced the observance of the festival you so lightly name to be of a highly superstitious nature? Your deceased mother, you were saying, will have entered into her reward forty years ago on February the second of next year? Is not this the case?"

"These forty years came Febbymas, I mean, and a good woman she was, and never have I seen a larger wart on the nose and her legs bad as bad for years and years!"

"These details, though, no doubt, of high personal interest, seem hardly germane to our present undertaking. However, Mrs. Belper, proceed in your remarks."

"And thank you kindly, Sir, and not forgetting you are a clergyman - but there! we can't all of us be everything. And my pore mother, as I was saying, Sir, she said, again and again, that if she'd been like some folks she'd a made a fortune in golden money from this very yarb I'm a-showing you, Sir."

"Dear me, Mrs. Belper! You interest me deeply. I have often thought how wrong it is of us to neglect, as undoubtedly we *do* neglect, the bounteous gifts of the kindly earth. Your lamented mother used this specific with remarkable success?"

"Lord a mercy, Doctor 'Chesson! elephants couldn't a stood against it, nor yet whales, being as how it's stronger than the strongest gunpowder that was ever brewed or blasted, and miles better than the nasty rubbidge you get in them doctors' shops, and a pretty penny they make you pay for it and no better than calomel, if you ask me, Sir. But be it the strongest of the strong, I'll take my Gospel oath it's weak to what my pore mother made, and that anybody in Much Moddle parish would tell you, for man, woman or child who took one of Mrs. Marjoram's Mixtures and got over it, remember it, he would, until his dying day. And my pore old mother, she was that funny - never was a cheerfuller woman, I do believe, and when Tom Copus, the lame fiddler, he got married, pore mother! though she could hardly walk, her legs was that bad, come she would, and if she didn't slip a little of the mixture into the beer when everybody was looking another way! Pore, dear soul! as she said herself afterwards, 'mirth becomes marriage,' and so to be sure it does, and merry they all were that day that didn't touch the beer, preferring spirits, which pore mother couldn't get at, being locked up - a nasty, mean trick, I call it, and always will."

"Enough, Mrs. Belper, enough! You have amply satisfied me as to the potency of the late Mrs. Marjoram's pharmacopoeia. We will, if you have no objection, Mrs. Belper, make the mixture - to use the words of Shakespeare - 'slab and thick.'"

"And bless your kind 'art, Sir, and a good, kind master you've always been to me, if you 'aven't got enough 'ere to lay out all the Lupton town, call me a Dutchwoman, and that I never was, nor pore Belper neither."

"Certainly not, Mrs. Belper. The Dutch belong to a different branch of the great Teutonic stock, or, if identity had ever existed, the two races have long been differentiated. I think, Mrs. Belper, that the most eminent physicians have recognised the beneficial effects of a gentle laxative during the treacherous (though delightful) season of spring?"

"Law bless you, Sir, you're right, as you always are, or why, Doctor? As my pore mother used to say when she made up the mixture: 'Scour 'em out is the right way about!' And laugh she would as she pounded the stuff up till I really thought she would 'a busted, and shaking like the best blancmanges all the while."

"Mrs. Belper, you have removed a weight from my mind. You think, then, that I shall be freed from all unfair competition while I pay my addresses to my young friend, Miss Floyer?"

"As free you will be, Doctor Chesson, Sir, as the little birds in the air; for not one of them young fellers will stand on his feet for days, and groans and 'owls will be the best word that mortal man will speak, and bless you they will with their dying breath. So, Sir, you'll 'ave the sweet young lady, bless her dear 'art, all to yourself, and if it's twins, don't blame me!"

"Mrs. Belper, your construction, if I may say so, is somewhat proleptic in its character. Still, I am sure that your meaning is good. Ha! I hear the bell for afternoon school."

The Doctor's voice happened to be shrill and piercing, with something of the tone of the tooth-comb and tissue-paper; while the fat cook spoke in a suety, husky contralto. Ambrose reproduced these peculiarities with the gift of the born mimic, adding appropriate antic and gesture to grace the show, and Nelly's appreciation of its humours was intense.

Day by day new incidents and scenes were added. The Head, in the pursuit of his guilty passion, hid in the coal-cellar of the "Bell," and, rustling sounds being heard, evaded detection for a while by imitating the barks of a terrier in chase of a rat. Nelly liked to hear the "Wuff! wuff! wuff!" which was introduced at this point. She liked also the final catastrophe, when the odd man of the "Bell" burst into the bar and said: "Dang my eyes, if it ain't the Doctor! I seed his cap and gown as he run round and round the coals on all fours, a-growling 'orrible." To which the landlady rejoined: "Don't tell your silly lies here! How *could* he growl, him being a clergyman?" And all the loafers joined in the chorus: "That's right, Tom; why *do* you talk such silly lies as that - him being a clergyman?"

They laughed so loud and so merrily over their morning tea and these lunacies that the landlady doubted gravely as to their marriage lines. She cared nothing; they had paid what she asked, money down in advance, and, as she said: "Young gentlemen *will* have their fun with the young ladies - so what's the good of talking?"

Breakfast came at length. They gave the landlady a warning bell some half-hour in advance, so the odd food was, at all events, not cold. Afterwards Nelly sallied off on her shopping expeditions, which, as might have been expected, she enjoyed hugely, and Ambrose stayed alone, with his pen and ink and a fat notebook which had captured his eye in a stationer's window.

Under these odd circumstances, then, he laid the foundations of his rare and precious *Defence of Taverns*, which is now termed by those fortunate enough to possess copies as a unique and golden treatise. Though he added a good deal in later years and remodelled and rearranged freely, there is a certain charm of vigour and freshness about the first sketch which is quite delightful in its way. Take, for example, the description of the whole world overwhelmed with sobriety: a deadly absence of inebriation annulling and destroying all the works and thoughts of men, the country itself at point to perish of the want of good liquor and good drinkers. He shows how there is grave cause to dread that, by reason of this sad neglect of the Dionysiac Mysteries, humanity is fast falling backward from the great heights to which it had ascended, and is in imminent danger of returning to the dumb and blind and helpless condition of the brutes.

"How else," he says, "can one account for the stricken state in which all the animal world grows and is eternally impotent? To them, strange, vast and enormous powers and faculties have been given. Consider, for example, the curious equipments of two odd extremes in this sphere - the ant and the elephant. The ant, if one may say so, is very near to us. We have our great centres of industry, our Black Country and our slaves who, if not born black, become black in our service. And the ants, too, have their black, enslaved races who do their dirty work for them, and are, perhaps, congratulated on their privileges as sharing in the blessings of civilisation - though this may be a refinement. The ant slaves, I believe, will rally eagerly to the defence of the nest and the eggs, and they say that the labouring classes are Liberal to the core. Nay; we grow mushrooms by art, and so they. In some lands, I think, they make enormous nests which are the nuisance and terror of the country. We have Manchester and Lupton and Leeds, and many such places - one would think them altogether civilised.

"The elephant, again, has many gifts which we lack. Note the curious instinct (or intuition, rather) of danger. The elephant knows, for example, when a bridge is unsafe, and refuses to pass, where a man would go on to destruction. One might examine in the same way all the creatures, and find in them singular capacities.

"Yet - they have no art. They see - but they see not. They hear - and they hear not. The odour in their nostrils has no sweetness at all. They have made no report of all the wonders that they knew. Their houses are, sometimes, as ingenious as a Chemical Works, but never is there any beauty for beauty's sake.

"It is clear that their state is thus desolate, because of the heavy pall of sobriety that hangs over them all; and it scarcely seems to have occurred to our 'Temperance' advocates that when they urge on us the example and abstinence of the beasts they have advanced the deadliest of all arguments against their nostrum. The Laughing Jackass is a teetotaller, doubtless, but no sane man should desire to be a Laughing Jackass.

"But the history of the men who have attained, who have done the glorious things of the earth and have become for ever exalted is the history of the men who have quested the Cup. Dionysius, said the Greeks, *civilised* the world; and the Bacchic Mystery was, naturally, the heart and core of Greek civilisation.

"Note the similitudes of Vine and Vineyard in Old Testament.

"Note the Quest of the San Graal.

"Note Rabelais and *La Dive Bouteille.*

"Place yourself in imagination in a Gothic Cathedral of the thirteenth century and assist at High Mass. Then go to the nearest Little Bethel, and look, and listen. Consider the difference in the two buildings, in those who worship in one and listen and criticise in the other. You have the difference between the Inebriated and the Sober, displayed in their works. As Little Bethel is to Tintern, so is Sobriety to Inebriation.

"Modern civilisation has advanced in many ways? Yes. Bethel has a stucco front. This material was quite unknown to the builders of Tintern Abbey. Advanced? What is advancement? Freedom from excesses, from extravagances, from wild enthusiasms? Small Protestant tradesmen are free from all these things, certainly. But is the joy of Adulteration to be the last goal, the final Initiation of the Race of Men? *Cœlumque tueri* - to sand the sugar?

"The Flagons of the Song of Songs did not contain ginger-beer.

"But the worst of it is we shall not merely descend to the beasts. We shall fall very far below the beasts. A black fellow is good, and a white fellow is good. But the white fellow who 'goes Fantee' does not become a negro - he becomes something infinitely worse, a horrible mass of the most putrid corruption.

"If we can clear our minds of the horrible cant of our 'civilisation,' if we can look at a modern 'industrial centre' with eyes purged of illusions, we shall have some notion of the awful horror to which we are descending in our effort to become as the ants and bees - creatures who know nothing of

CALIX INEBRIANS.

"I doubt if we can really make this effort. Blacks, Stinks, Desolations, Poisons, Hell's Nightmare generally have, I suspect, worked themselves into the very form and mould of our thoughts. We are sober, and perhaps the Tavern door is shut for ever against us.

"Now and then, perhaps, at rarer and still rarer intervals, a few of us will hear very faintly the far echoes of the holy madness within the closed door:

> *"When up the thyrse is raised, and when the sound Of sacred orgies flies 'around, around.'*

"Which is the *Sonus Epulantium in Æterno Convivio.*

"But this we shall not be able to discern. Very likely we shall take the noise of this High Choir for the horrid mirth of Hell. How strange it is that those who are pledged officially and ceremonially, as it were, to a Rite of Initiation which figures certainly a Feast, should in all their thoughts and words and actions be continually blaspheming and denying all the uses and ends of feastings and festivals.

"This is not the refusal of the *species* for the sake of enjoying perfectly the most beautiful and desirable *genus*; it is the renouncing of species and genus, the pronouncing of Good to be Evil. The Universal being denied, the Particular is degraded and defiled. What is called 'The Drink Curse' is the natural and inevitable result and sequence of the 'Protestant Reformation.' If the clear wells and fountains of the magic wood are buried out of sight, then men (who must have Drink) will betake them to the Slime Ponds and Poison Pools.

"In the Graal Books there is a curse - an evil enchantment - on the land of Logres because the mystery of the Holy Vessel is disregarded. The Knight sees the Dripping Spear and the Shining Cup pass before him, and says no word. He asks no question as to the end and meaning of this ceremony. So the land is blasted and barren and songless, and those who dwell in it are in misery.

"Every day of our lives we see the Graal carried before us in a wonderful order, and every day we leave the question unasked, the Mystery despised and neglected. Yet if we could ask that question, bowing down before these Heavenly and Glorious Splendours and Hallows - then every man should have the meat and drink that his soul desired; the hall would be filled with odours of Paradise, with the light of Immortality.

"In the books the Graal was at last taken away because of men's unworthiness. So it will be, I suppose. Even now, the Quester's adventure is a desperate one - few there be that find It.

"Ventilation and sanitation are well enough in their way. But it would not be very satisfactory to pass the day in a ventilated and sanitated Hell with nothing to eat or drink. If one is perishing of hunger and thirst, sanitation seems unimportant enough.

"How wonderful, how glorious it would be if the Kingdom of the Great Drinkers could be restored! If we could only sweep away all the might of the Sober Ones - the factory builders, the poison makers, the politicians, the manufacturers of bad books and bad pictures, together with Little Bethel and the morality of Mr. Mildmay, the curate (a series of negative propositions) - then imagine the Great Light of the Great Inebriation shining on every face, and not any work of man's hands, from a cathedral to a penknife, without the mark of the Tavern upon it! All the world a great festival; every well a fountain of strong drink; every river running with the New Wine; the Sangraal brought back from Sarras, restored to the awful shrine of Cor-arbennic, the Oracle of the *Dive Bouteille* once more freely given, the ruined Vineyard flourishing once more, girt about by shining, everlasting walls! Then we should hear the Old Songs again, and they would dance the Old Dances, the happy, ransomed people, Commensals and Compotators of the Everlasting Tavern."

The whole treatise, of which this extract is a fragment in a rudimentary and imperfect stage, is, of course, an impassioned appeal for the restoration of the quickening, exuberant imagination, not merely in art, but in all the inmost places of life. There is more than this, too. Here and there one can hear, as it were, the whisper and the hint of deeper mysteries, visions of a great experiment and a great achievement to which some men may be called. In his own words: "Within the Tavern there is an Inner Tavern, but the door of it is visible to few indeed."

In Ambrose's mind in the after years the stout notebook was dear, perhaps as a substitute for that aroma of the past in a phial which he has declared so desirable an invention. It stood, not so much for what was written in it as for the place and the circumstances in which it was written. It recalled Little Russell Row and Nelly, and the evenings at the Château de Chinon, where, night by night, they served still stranger, more delicious meats, and the red wine revealed more clearly its high celestial origin. One evening was diversified by an odd encounter.

A middle-aged man, sitting at an adjoining table, was evidently in want of matches, and Ambrose handed his box with the sympathetic smile which one smoker gives to another in such cases. The man - he had a black moustache and a small, pointed beard - thanked him in fluent English with a French accent, and they began to talk of casual things, veering, by degrees, in the direction of the arts. The Frenchman smiled at Meyrick's enthusiasm.

"What a life you have before you!" he said. "Don't you know that the populace always hates the artist - and kills him if it can? You are an artist and mystic, too. What a fate!

"Yes; but it is that applause, that *réclame* that comes after the artist is dead," he went on, replying to some objection of Ambrose's; "it is that which is the worst cruelty of all. It is fine for Burns, is it not, that his stupid compatriots have not ceased to utter follies about him for the last eighty years? Scotchmen? But they should be ashamed to speak his name! And Keats, and how many others in my country and in yours and in all countries? The imbeciles are not content to calumniate, to persecute, to make wretched the artist in his lifetime. They follow him with their praise to the grave - the grave that they have digged! Praise of the populace! Praise of a race of pigs! For, you see, while they are insulting the dead with their compliments they are at the same time insulting the living with their abuse."

He dropped into silence; from his expression he seemed to be cursing "the populace" with oaths too frightful to be uttered. He rose suddenly and turned to Ambrose.

"Artist - and mystic. Yes. You will probably be crucified. Good evening ... and a fine martyrdom to you!"

He was gone with a charming smile and a delightful bow to "Madame." Ambrose looked after him with a puzzled face; his last words had called up some memory that he could not capture; and then suddenly he recollected the old, ragged Irish fiddler, the player of strange fantasies under the tree in the outskirts of Lupton. He thought of his phrase about "red martyrdom"; it was an odd coincidence.

IV

The phrases kept recurring to his mind after they had gone out, and as they wandered through the lighted streets with all their strange and variegated show, with glittering windows and glittering lamps, with the ebb and flow of faces, the voices and the laughter, the surging crowds about the theatre doors, the flashing hansoms and the omnibuses lumbering heavily along to strange regions, such as Turnham Green and Castlenau, Cricklewood and Stoke Newington - why, they were as unknown as cities in Cathay!

It was a dim, hot night; all the great city smoked as with a mist, and a tawny moon rose through films of cloud far in the vista of the east. Ambrose thought with a sudden recollection that the moon, that world of splendour, was shining in a farther land, on the coast of the wild rocks, on the heaving sea, on the faery apple-garths in Avalon, where, though the apples are always golden, yet the blossoms of enchantment never fade, but hang for ever against the sky.

They were passing a half-lit street, and these dreams were broken by the sudden clanging, rattling music of a piano-organ. For a moment they saw the shadowy figures of the children as they flitted to and fro, dancing odd measures in the rhythm of the tune. Then they came into a long, narrow way with a church spire in the distance, and near the church they passed the "church-shop" - Roman, evidently, from the subjects and the treatment of the works of art on view. But it was strange! In the middle of the window was a crude, glaring statue of some saint. He was in bright red robes, sprinkled with golden stars; the blood rained down from a wound in his forehead, and with one hand he drew the scarlet vestment aside and pointed to the dreadful gash above his heart, and from this, again, the bloody drops fell thick. The colours stared and shrieked, and yet, through the bad, cheap art there seemed to shine a rapture that was very near to beauty; the thing expressed was so great that it had to a certain extent overcome the villainy of the expression.

They wandered vaguely, after their custom. Ambrose was silent; he was thinking of Avalon and "Red Martyrdom" and the Frenchman's parting salutation, of the vision in one of the old books, "the Man clothed in a robe redder and more shining than burning fire, and his feet and his hands and his face were of a like flame, and five angels in fiery vesture stood about him, and at the feet of the Man the ground was covered with a ruddy dew."

They passed under an old church tower that rose white in the moonlight above them. The air had cleared, the mist had floated away, and now the sky glowed violet, and the white stones of the classic spirit shone on high. From it there came suddenly a tumult of glad sound, exultant bells in ever-changing order, pealing out as if to honour some great victory, so that the mirth of the street below became but a trivial restless noise. He thought of some passage that he had read but could not distinctly remember: a ship was coming back to its haven after a weary and tempestuous voyage over many dreadful seas, and those on board saw the tumult in the city as their sails were sighted; heard afar the shouts of gladness from the rejoicing people; heard the bells from all the spires and towers break suddenly into triumphant chorus, sounding high above the washing of the waves.

Ambrose roused himself from his dreams. They had been walking in a circle and had returned almost to the street of the Château, though, their knowledge of the district being of an unscientific character, they were under the impression that they were a mile or so away from that particular point. As it happened, they had not entered this street before, and they were charmed at the sudden appearance of stained glass lighted up from within. The colour was rich and good; there were flourished scrolls and grotesques in the Renaissance manner, many emblazoned shields in ruby and gold and azure; and the centre-piece showed the Court of the Beer King - a jovial and venerable figure attended by a host of dwarfs and kobolds, all holding on high enormous mugs of beer. They went in boldly and were glad. It was the famous "Three Kings" in its golden and unreformed days, but this they knew not. The room was of moderate size, very low, with great dark beams in the white ceiling. White were the walls; on the plaster, black-letter texts with vermilion initials praised the drinker's art, and more kobolds, in black and red, loomed oddly in unsuspected corners. The lighting, presumably, was gas, but all that was visible were great antique lanterns depending from iron hooks, and through their dull green glass only a dim radiance fell upon the heavy oak tables and the drinkers. From the middle beam an enormous bouquet of fresh hops hung on high; there was a subdued murmur of talk, and now and then the clatter of the lid of a mug, as fresh beer was ordered. In one corner there was a kind of bar; behind it a couple of grim women - the kobolds apparently - performed their office; and above, on a sort of rack, hung mugs and tankards of all sizes and of all fantasies. There were plain mugs of creamy earthenware, mugs gaudily and oddly painted with garlanded goats, with hunting scenes, with towering castles, with flaming posies of flowers. Then some friend of the drunken, some sage who had pried curiously into the secrets of thirst, had made a series of wonders in glass, so shining and crystalline that to behold them was as if one looked into a well, for every glitter of the facets gave promise of satisfaction. There were the mugs, capacious and very deep, crowned for the most part not with mere plain lids of common use and make, but with tall spires in pewter, richly ornamented, evident survivals from the Middle Ages. Ambrose's eyes glistened; the place was altogether as he would have designed it. Nelly, too, was glad to sit down, for they had walked longer than usual. She was refreshed by a glass of some cool drink with a borage flower and a cherry floating in it, and Ambrose ordered a mug of beer.

It is not known how many of these krugs he emptied. It was, as has been noted, a sultry night, and the streets were dusty, and that glass of Benedictine after dinner rather evokes than dismisses the demon of thirst. Still, Munich beer is no hot and rebellious drink, so the causes of what followed must probably be sought for in other springs. Ambrose took a deep draught, gazed upward to the ceiling, and ordered another mug of beer for himself and some more of the cool and delicate and flowery beverage for Nelly. When the drink was set upon the board, he thus began, without title or preface:

"You must know, Nelly dear," he said, "that the marriage of Panurge, which fell out in due time (according to the oracle and advice of the Holy Bottle), was by no means a fortunate one. For, against all the counsel of Pantagruel and of Friar John, and indeed of all his friends, Panurge married in a fit of spleen and obstinacy the crooked and squinting daughter of the little old man who sold green sauce in the Rue Quincangrogne at Tours - you will see the very place in a few days, and then you will understand everything. You do not understand that? My child, that is impiety, since it accuses the Zeitgest, who is certainly the only god that ever existed, as you will see more fully demonstrated in Huxley and Spencer and all the leading articles in all the leading newspapers. *Quod erat demonstrandum*. To be still more precise: You must know that when I am dead, and a very great man indeed, many thousands of people will come from all the quarters of the globe - not forgetting the United States - to Lupton. They will come and stare very hard at the Old Grange, which will have an inscription about me on the wall; they will spend hours in High School; they will walk all round Playing Fields; they will cut little bits off 'brooks' and 'quarries.' Then they will view the Sulphuric Acid works, the Chemical Manure factory and the Free Library, and whatever other stink-pots and cesspools Lupton town may contain; they will finally enjoy the view of the Midland Railway Goods Station. Then they will say: '*Now* we understand him; *now* one sees how he got all his inspiration in that lovely old school and the wonderful English country-side.' So you see that when I show you the Rue Quincangrogne you will perfectly understand this history. Let us drink; the world shall never be drowned again, so have no fear.

"Well, the fact remains that Panurge, having married this hideous wench aforesaid, was excessively unhappy. It was in vain that he argued with his wife in all known languages and in some that are unknown, for, as she said, she only knew two languages, the one of Touraine and the other of the Stick, and this second she taught Panurge *per modum passionis* - that is by beating him, and this so thoroughly that poor Pilgarlic was sore from head to foot. He was a worthy little fellow, but the greatest coward that ever breathed. Believe me, illustrious

112

drinkers and most precious.... Nelly, never was man so wretched as this Panurge since Paradise fell from Adam. This is the true doctrine; I heard it when I was at Eleusis. You enquire what was the matter? Why, in the first place, this vile wretch whom they all called - so much did they hate her - La Vie Mortale, or Deadly Life, this vile wretch, I say: what do you think that she did when the last note of the fiddles had sounded and the wedding guests had gone off to the 'Three Lampreys' to kill a certain worm - the which worm is most certainly immortal, since it is not dead yet! Well, then, what did Madame Panurge? Nothing but this: She robbed her excellent and devoted husband of all that he had. Doubtless you remember how, in the old days, Panurge had played ducks and drakes with the money that Pantagruel had given him, so that he borrowed on his corn while it was still in the ear, and before it was sown, if we enquire a little more closely. In truth, the good little man never had a penny to bless himself withal, for the which cause Pantagruel loved him all the more dearly. So that when the Dive Bouteille gave its oracle, and Panurge chose his spouse, Pantagruel showed how preciously he esteemed a hearty spender by giving him such a treasure that the goldsmiths who live under the bell of St. Gatien still talk of it before they dine, because by doing so their mouths water, and these salivary secretions are of high benefit to the digestion: read on this, Galen. If you would know how great and glorious this treasure was, you must go to the Library of the Archevêché at Tours, where they will show you a vast volume bound in pigskin, the name of which I have forgotten. But this book is nothing else than the list of all the wonders and glories of Pantagruel's wedding present to Panurge; it contains surprising things, I can tell you, for, in good coin of the realm alone, never was gift that might compare with it; and besides the common money there were ancient pieces, the very names of which are now incomprehensible, and incomprehensible they will remain till the coming of the Coqcigrues. There was, for instance, a great gold Sol, a world in itself, as some said truly, and I know not how many myriad myriad of Étoiles, all of the finest silver that was ever minted, and Anges-Gardiens, which the learned think must have been first coined at Angers, though others will have it that they were the same as our Angels; and, as for Roses de Paradis and Couronnes Immortelles, I believe he had as many of them as ever he would. Beauties and joys he was to keep for pocket-money; small change is sometimes great gain. And, as I say, no sooner had Panurge married that accursed daughter of the Rue Quincangrogne than she robbed him of everything, down to the last brass farthing. The fact is that the woman was a witch; she was also something else which I leave out for the present. But, if you will believe me, she cast such a spell upon Panurge that he thought himself an absolute beggar. Thus he would look at his Sol d'Or and say: 'What is the use of that? It is only a great bright lump: I can see it every day.' Then when they said, 'But how about those Anges-Gardiens?' he would reply, 'Where are they? Have you seen them? I never see them. Show them to me,' and so with all else; and all the while that villain of a woman beat, thumped and belaboured him so that the tears were always in his eyes, and they say you could hear him howling all over the world. Everybody said that he had made a pretty mess of it, and would come to a bad end.

"Luckily for him, this ... witch of a wife of his would sometimes doze off for a few minutes, and then he had a little peace, and he would wonder what had become of all the gay girls and gracious ladies that he had known in old times - for he had played the devil with the women in his day and could have taught Ovid lessons in *arte amoris*. Now, of course, it was as much as his life was worth to mention the very name of one of these ladies, and as for any little sly visits, stolen endearments, hidden embraces, or any small matters of that kind, it was *good-bye, I shall see you next Nevermas*. Nor was this all, but worse remains behind; and it is my belief that it is the thought of what I am going to tell you that makes the wind wail and cry of winter nights, and the clouds weep, and the sky look black; for in truth it is the greatest sorrow that ever was since the beginning of the world. I must out with it quick, or I shall never have done: in plain English, and as true as I sit here drinking good ale, not one drop or minim or drachm or pennyweight of drink had Panurge tasted since the day of his wedding! He had implored mercy, he had told her how he had served Gargantua and Pantagruel and had got into the habit of drinking in his sleep, and his wife had merely advised him to go to the devil - she was not going to let him so much as look at the nasty stuff. '"Touch not, taste not, smell not," is my motto,' said she. She gave him a blue ribbon, which she said would make up for it. 'What do you want with Drink?' said she. 'Go and do business instead, it's much better for you.'

"Sad, then, and sorry enough was the estate of poor Panurge. At last, so wretched did he become, that he took advantage of one of his wife's dozes and stole away to the good Pantagruel, and told him the whole story - and a very bad one it was - so that the tears rolled down Pantagruel's cheeks from sheer grief, and each teardrop contained exactly one hundred and eighteen gallons of aqueous fluid, according to the calculations of the best geometers. The great man saw that the case was a desperate one, and Heaven knew, he said, whether it could be mended or not; but certain it was that a business such as this could not be settled in a hurry, since it was not like a game at shove-ha'penny to be got over between two gallons of wine. He therefore counselled Panurge to have patience and bear with his wife for a few thousand years, and in the meantime they would see what could be done. But, lest his patience should wear out, he gave him an odd drug or medicine, prepared by the great artist of the Mountains of Cathay, and this he was to drop into his wife's glass - for though he might have no drink, she was drunk three times a day, and she would sleep all the longer, and leave him awhile in peace. This Panurge very faithfully performed, and got a little rest now and again, and they say that while that devil of a woman snored and snorted he was able, by odd chances once or twice, to get hold of a drop of the right stuff - good old Stingo from the big barrel - which he lapped up as eagerly as a kitten laps cream. Others there be who declare that once or twice he got about his sad old tricks, while his ugly wife was sleeping in the sun; the women on the Maille make no secret of their opinion that his old mistress, Madame Sophia, was seen stealing in and out of the house as slyly as you please, and God knows what goes on when the door is shut. But the Tourainians were always sad gossips, and one must not believe all that one hears. I leave out the flat scandal-mongers who are bold enough to declare that he kept one mistress at Jerusalem, another at Eleusis, another in Egypt and about as many as are contained in the seraglio of the Grand Turk, scattered up and down in the towns and villages of Asia; but I do believe there was some kissing in dark corners, and a curtain hung across one room in the house could tell odd tales. Nevertheless, La Vie Mortale (a pest on her!) was more often awake than asleep, and when she was awake Panurge's case was worse than ever. For, you see, the woman was no piece of a fool, and she saw sure enough that something was going on. The Stingo in the barrel was lower than of rights, and more than once she had caught her husband looking almost happy, at which she beat the house about his ears. Then, another time, Madame Sophia dropped her ring, and again this sweet lady came one morning so strongly perfumed that she scented the whole place, and when La Vie woke up it smelt like a church. There was fine work then, I promise you; the people heard the bangs and curses and shrieks and groans as far as Amboise on the one side and Luynes on the other; and that year the Loire rose ten feet higher than the banks on account of Panurge's tears. As a punishment, she made him go and be industrial, and he built ten thousand stink-pot factories with twenty thousand chimneys, and all the leaves and trees and green grass and flowers in the world were blackened and died, and all the waters were poisoned so that there were no perch in the Loire, and salmon fetched forty sols the pound at Chinon market. As for the men and women, they became yellow apes and listened to a codger named Calvin, who told them they would all be damned eternally (except himself and his friends), and they found his doctrine very comforting, and probable too, since they had the sense to know that they were more than half damned already. I don't know whether Panurge's fate was worse on this occasion or on another when his wife found a book in his writing, full from end to end of poetry; some of it about the wonderful treasure that Pantagruel had given him, which he was supposed to have forgotten. Some of it verses to those old light-o'-loves of his, with a whole epic in praise of his mistress-in-chief, Sophia. Then, indeed, there was the very deuce to pay; it was bread and water, stripes and torment, all day long, and La Vie swore a great oath that if he ever did it again he should be sent to spend the rest of his life in Manchester, whereupon he fell into a swoon from horrid fright and lay like a log, so that everybody thought he was dead.

"All this while the great Pantagruel was not idle. Perceiving how desperate the matter was, he summoned the Thousand and First Great Œcumenical Council of all the sages of the wide world, and when the fathers had come, and had heard High Mass at St. Gatien's, the session was opened in a pavilion in the meadows by the Loire just under the Lanterne of Roche Corbon, whence this Council is always styled the great and holy Council of the Lantern. If you want to know where the place is you can do so very easily, for there is a choice tavern on the spot where the pavilion stood, and there you may have *malelotte* and *friture* and amber wine of Vouvray, better than in any tavern in Touraine. As for the history of the acts of this great Council, it is still a-writing, and so far only two thousand volumes in elephant folio have been printed *sub signo Lucernæ cum permissu superiorum*. However, as it is necessary to be brief, it may be said that the holy fathers of the Lantern, after having heard the whole case as it was exposed to them by the great clerks of Pantagruel, having digested all the arguments, looked into the precedents, applied themselves to the doctrine, explored the hidden wisdom, consulted the Canons, searched the Scriptures, divided the dogma, distinguished the distinctions and answered the questions, resolved with one voice that there was no help in the world for Panurge, save only this: he must forthwith achieve the most high, noble and glorious quest of the Sangraal, for no other way was there under heaven by which he might rid himself of that pestilent wife of his, La Vie Mortale.

"And on some other occasion," said Ambrose, "you may hear of the last voyage of Panurge to the Glassy Isle of the Holy Graal, of the incredible adventures that he achieved, of the dread perils through which he passed, of the great wonders and marvels and compassions of the way, of the manner in which he received the title Plentyn y Tonau, which signifies 'Child of the Waterfloods,' and how at last he gloriously attained the vision of the Sangraal, and was most happily translated out of the power of La Vie Mortale."

"And where is he now?" said Nelly, who had found the tale interesting but obscure.

"It is not precisely known - opinions vary. But there are two odd things: one is that he is exactly like that man in the red dress whose statue we saw in the shop window to-night; and the other is that from that day to this he has never been sober for a single minute.

> *"Calix meus inebrians quam præclarus est!"*

V

Ambrose took a great draught from the mug and emptied it, and forthwith rapped the lid for a fresh supply. Nelly was somewhat nervous; she was afraid he might begin to sing, for there were extravagances in the history of Panurge which seemed to her to be of alcoholic source. However, he did not sing; he lapsed into silence, gazing at the dark beams, the hanging hops, the bright array of the tankards and the groups of drinkers dotted about the room. At a neighbouring table two Germans were making a hearty meal, chumping the meat and smacking their lips in a kind of heavy ecstasy. He had but little German, but he caught scraps of the conversation.

One man said:

"Heavenly swine cutlets!"

And the other answered:

"Glorious eating!"

"Nelly," said Ambrose, "I have a great inspiration!"

She trembled visibly.

"Yes; I have talked so much that I am hungry. We will have some supper."

They looked over the list of strange eatables and, with the waiter's help, decided on Leberwurst and potato-salad as light and harmless. With this they ate crescent loaves, sprinkled with caraway seeds: there was more Munich Lion-Brew and more flowery drink, with black coffee, a fine and a Maraschino to end all. For Nelly the kobolds began to perform a grotesque and mystic dance in the shadows, the glass tankards on the rack glittered strangely, the white walls with the red and black texts retreated into vast distances, and the bouquet of hops seemed suspended from a remote star. As for Ambrose, he was certainly not *ebrius* according to the Baron's definition; he was hardly *ebriolus*; but he was sensible, let us say, of a certain quickening of the fancy, of a more vivid and poignant enjoyment of the whole situation, of the unutterable gaiety of this mad escape from the conventions of Lupton.

"It was a Thursday night," said Ambrose in the after years, "and we were thinking of starting for Touraine either the next morning or on Saturday at latest. It will always be bright in my mind, that picture - the low room with the oak beams, the glittering tankards, the hops hanging from the ceiling, and Nelly sitting before me sipping the scented drink from a green glass. It was the last night of gaiety, and even then gaiety was mixed with odd patterns - the Frenchman's talk about martyrdom, and the statue of the saint pointing to the marks of his passion, standing in that dyed vesture with his rapt, exultant face; and then the song of final triumph and deliverance that rang out on the chiming bells from the white spire. I think the contrast of this solemn undertone made my heart all the lighter; I was in that odd state in which one delights to know that one is not being understood - so I told poor Nelly 'the story of Panurge's marriage to La Vie Mortale; I am sure she thought I was drunk!

"We went home in a hansom, and agreed that we would have just one cigarette and then go to bed. It was settled that we would catch the night boat to Dieppe on the next day, and we both laughed with joy at the thought of the adventure. And then - I don't know how it was - Nelly began to tell me all about herself. She had never said a word before; I had never asked her - I never ask anybody about their past lives. What does it matter? You know a certain class of plot - novelists are rather fond of using it - in which the hero's happiness is blasted because he finds out that the life of his wife or his sweetheart has not always been spotless as the snow. Why should it be spotless as the snow? What is the hero that he should be dowered with the love of virgins of Paradise? I call it cant - all that - and I hate it; I hope Angel Clare was eventually entrapped by a young person from Piccadilly Circus - she would probably be much too good for him! So, you see, I was hardly likely to have put any very searching questions to Nelly; we had other things to talk about.

"But this night I suppose she was a bit excited. It had been a wild and wonderful week. The transition from that sewage-pot in the Midlands to the Abbey of Theleme was enough to turn any head; we had laughed till we had grown dizzy. The worst of that miserable school discipline is is that it makes one take an insane and quite disproportionate enjoyment in little things, in the merest trifles which ought really to be accepted as a matter of course. I assure you that every minute that I spent in bed after seven o'clock was to me a grain of Paradise, a moment of delight. Of course, it's ridiculous; let a man get up early or get up late, as he likes or as he finds best - and say no more about it. But at that wretched Lupton early rising was part of the infernal blether and blatter of the place, that made life there like a long dinner in which every dish has the same sauce. It may be a good sauce enough; but one is sick of the taste of it. According to our Bonzes there, getting up early on a winter's day was a high virtue which acquired merit. I believe I should have liked a hard chair to sit in of my own free will, if one of our old fools - Palmer - had not always been gabbling about the horrid luxury of some boys who had arm-chairs in their studies. Unless you were doing something or other to make yourself very uncomfortable, he used to say you were like the 'later Romans.' I am sure he believed that those lunatics who bathe in the Serpentine on Christmas Day would go straight to heaven!

"And there you are. I would awake at seven o'clock from persistent habit, and laugh as I realised that I was in Little Russell Row and not at the Old Grange. Then I would doze off again and wake up at intervals - eight, nine, ten - and chuckle to myself with ever-increasing enjoyment. It was just the same with smoking. I don't suppose I should have touched a cigarette for years if smoking had not been one of the mortal sins in our Bedlam Decalogue. I don't know whether smoking is bad for boys or not; I should think not, as I believe the Dutch - who are sturdy fellows - begin to puff fat cigars at the age of six or thereabouts; but I do know that those pompous old boobies and blockheads and leather-skulls have discovered exactly the best way to make a boy think that a packet of Rosebuds represents the quintessence of frantic delight.

"Well, you see how it was, how Little Russell Row - the dingy, the stuffy, the dark retreat of old Bloomsbury - became the abode of miraculous joys, a bright portion of fairyland. Ah! it was a strong new wine that we tasted, and it went to our heads, and not much wonder. It all rose to its height on that Thursday night when we went to the 'Three Kings' and sat beneath the hop bush, drinking Lion-Brew and flowery drink as I talked extravagances concerning Panurge. It was time for the curtain to be rung down on our comedy.

"The one cigarette had become three or four when Nelly began to tell me her history; the wine and the rejoicing had got into her head also. She described the first things that she remembered: a little hut among wild hills and stony fields in the west of Ireland, and the great sea roaring on the shore but a mile away, and the wind and the rain always driving from across the waves. She spoke of the place as if she loved it, though her father and mother were as poor as they could be, and little was there to eat even in the old cabin. She remembered Mass in the little chapel, an old, old place hidden way in the most desolate part of the country, small and dark and bare enough except for the candles on the altar and a bright statue or two. St. Kieran's cell, they called it, and it was supposed that the Mass had never ceased to be said there even in the blackest days of persecution. Quite well she remembered the old priest and his vestments, and the gestures that he used, and how they all bowed down when the bell rang; she could imitate his quavering voice saying the Latin. Her own father, she said, was a learned man in his way, though it was not the English way. He could not read common print, or write; he knew nothing about printed books, but he could say a lot of the old Irish songs and stories by heart, and he had sticks on which he wrote poems on all sorts of things, cutting notches on the wood in Oghams, as the priest called them; and he could tell many wonderful tales of the saints and the people. It was a happy life altogether; they were as poor as poor could be, and praised God and wanted for nothing. Then her mother went into a decline and died, and her father never lifted up his head again, and she was left an orphan when she was nine years old. The priest had written to an aunt who lived in England, and so she found herself one black day standing on the platform of the station in a horrible little manufacturing village in Lancashire; everything was black - the sky and the earth, and the houses and the people; and the sound of their rough, harsh voices made her sick. And the aunt had married an Independent and turned Protestant, so she was black, too, Nelly thought. She was wretched for a long time, she said. The aunt was kind enough to her, but the place and the people were so awful. Mr. Deakin, the husband, said he couldn't encourage Popery in his house, so she had to go to the meeting-house on Sunday and listen to the nonsense they called 'religion' - all long sermons with horrible shrieking hymns. By degrees she forgot her old prayers, and she was taken to the Dissenters' Sunday School, where they learned texts and heard about King Solomon's Temple, and Jonadab the son of Rechab, and Jezebel, and the Judges. They seemed to think a good deal of her at the school; she had several prizes for Bible knowledge.

"She was sixteen when she first went out to service. She was glad to get away - nothing could be worse than Farnworth, and it might be better. And then there were tales to tell! I never have had a clearer light thrown on the curious and disgusting manners of the lower middle-class in England - the class that prides itself especially on its respectability, above all, on what it calls 'Morality' - by which it means the observance of one particular commandment. You know the class I mean: the brigade of the shining hat on Sunday, of the neat little villa with a well-kept plot in front, of the consecrated drawing-room, of the big Bible well in evidence. It is more often Chapel than Church, this tribe, but it draws from both sources. It is above all things shiny - not only the Sunday hat, but the furniture, the linoleum, the hair and the very flesh which pertain to these people have an unwholesome polish on them; and they prefer their plants and shrubs to be as glossy as possible - this *gens lubrica*.

"To these tents poor Nelly went as a slave; she dwelt from henceforth on the genteel outskirts of more or less prosperous manufacturing towns, and she soon profoundly regretted the frank grime and hideousness of Farnworth. A hedgehog is a rough and prickly fellow - better his prickles than the reptile's poisonous slime. The tales that yet await the novelist who has courage (what is his name, by the way?), who has the insight to see behind those Venetian blinds and white curtains, who has the word that can give him entrance through the polished door by the encaustic porch! What plots, what pictures, what characters are ready for his cunning hand, what splendid matter lies unknown, useless, and indeed offensive, which, in the artist's crucible, would be transmuted into golden and exquisite perfection. Do you know that I can never penetrate into the regions where these people dwell without a thrill of wonder and a great desire that I might be called to execute the masterpieces I have hinted at? Do you remember how Zola, viewing these worlds from the train when he visited London, groaned because he had no English, because he had no key to open the treasure-house before his eyes? He, of course, who was a great diviner, saw the infinite variety of romance that was concealed beneath those myriads of snug commonplace roofs: I wish he could have observed in English and recorded in French. He was a brave man, his defence of Dreyfus shows that; but, supposing the capacity, I do not think he was brave enough to tell the London suburbs the truth about themselves in their own tongue.

"Yes, I walk down these long ways on Sunday afternoons, when they are at their best. Sometimes, if you choose the right hour, you may look into one 'breakfast room' - an apartment half sunken in the earth - after another, and see in each one the table laid for tea, showing the charming order and uniformity that prevail. Tea in the drawing-room would be, I suppose, a desecration. I wonder what would happen if some chance guest were to refuse tea and to ask for a glass of beer, or even a brandy and soda? I suppose the central lake that lies many hundreds of feet beneath London would rise up, and the sinful town would be overwhelmed. Yes: consider these houses well; how demure, how well-ordered, how shining, as I have said; and then think of what they conceal.

"Generally speaking, you know, 'morality' (in the English suburban sense) has been a tolerably equal matter. I shouldn't imagine that those 'later Romans' that poor old Palmer was always bothering about were much better or worse than the earlier Babylonians; and London as a whole is very much the same thing in this respect as Pekin as a whole. Modern Berlin and sixteenth-century Venice might compete on equal terms - save that Venice, I am sure, was very picturesque, and Berlin, I have no doubt is very piggy. The fact is, of course (to use a simple analogy), man, by his nature, is always hungry, and, that being the case, he will sometimes eat too much dinner and sometimes he will get his dinner in odd ways, and sometimes he will help himself to more or less unlawful snacks before breakfast and after supper. There it is, and there is an end of it. But suppose a society in which the fact of hunger was officially denied, in which the faintest hint at an empty stomach was considered the rankest, most abominable indecency, the most detestable offence against the most sacred religious feelings? Suppose the child severely reprimanded at the mere mention of bread and butter, whipped and shut up in a dark room for the offence of reading a recipe for making plum pudding; suppose, I say, a whole society organised on the strict official understanding that no decent person ever is or has been or can be conscious of the physical want of food; that breakfast, lunch, tea, dinner and supper are orgies only used by the most wicked and degraded wretches, destined to an awful and eternal doom? In such a world, I think, you would discover some very striking irregularities in diet. Facts are known to be stubborn things, but if their very existence is denied they become ferocious and terrible things. Coventry Patmore was angry, and with reason, when he heard that even at the Vatican the statues had received the order of the fig-leaf.

"Nelly went among these Manichees. She had been to the world beyond the Venetians, the white muslin curtains and the india-rubber plant, and she told me her report. They talk about the morality of the theatre, these swine! In the theatre - if there is anything of the kind - it is a case of a wastrel and a wanton who meet and part on perfectly equal terms, without deceit or false pretences. It is not a case of master creeping into a young girl's room at dead of night, with a Bible under his arm - the said Bible being used with grotesque skill to show that 'master's' wishes must be at once complied with under pain of severe punishment, not only in this world, but in the world to come. Every Sunday, you must remember, the girl has seen 'master' perhaps crouching devoutly in his pew, perhaps in the part of sidesman or even church-warden, more probably supplementing the gifts of the pastor at some nightmarish meeting-house. 'Master' offers prayer with wonderful fervour; he speaks to the Lord as man to man; in the emotional passages his voice gets husky, and everybody says how good he is. He is a deacon, a guardian of the poor (gracious title!), a builder and an earnest supporter of the British and Foreign Bible Society: in a word, he is of the great middle-class, the backbone of England and of the Protestant Religion. He subscribes to the excellent society which prosecutes booksellers for selling the Decameron of Boccaccio. He has from ten to fifteen children, all of whom were found by Mamma in the garden.

"'Mr. King was a horrible man,' said Nelly, describing her first place; 'he had a great greasy pale face with red whiskers, and a shiny bald head; he was fat, too, and when he smiled it made one feel sick. Soon after I got the place he came into the kitchen. Missus was away for three days, and the children were all in bed. He sat down by the hearth and asked whether I was saved, and did I love the Lord as I ought to, and if I ever had any bad thoughts about young men? Then he opened the Bible and read me nasty things from the Old Testament, and asked if I understood what it meant. I said I didn't know, and he said we must approach the Lord in prayer so that we might have grace to search the Scriptures together. I had to kneel down close to him, and he put his arm round my waist and began to pray, as he called it; and when we got up he took me on his knee and said he felt to me as if I were his own daughter.'

"There, that is enough of Mr. King. You can imagine what the poor child had to go through time after time. On prayer-meeting nights she used to put the chest of drawers against her bedroom door: there would be gentle, cautious pushes, and then a soft voice murmuring: 'My child, why is your heart so bad and stubborn?' I think we can conceive the general character of 'master' from these examples. 'Missus,' of course, requires a treatise to herself; her more frequent failings are child-torture, secret drinking and low amours with oily commercial travellers.

"Yes, it is a hideous world enough, isn't it? And isn't it a pleasant thought that you and I practically live under the government of these people? 'Master' is the 'man in the street,' the 'hard-headed, practical man of the world,' 'the descendant of the sturdy Puritans,' whose judgment is final on all questions from Poetics to Liturgiology. We hardly think that this picture will commend itself to the 'man in the street' - a course of action that is calculated to alienate practical men. Pleasant, isn't it? *Suburbia locuta est: causa finita est.*

"I suppose that, by nature, these people would not be so very much more depraved than the ordinary African black fellow. Their essential hideousness comes, I take it, from their essential and most abominable hypocrisy. You know how they are always prating about Bible Teaching - the 'simple morality of the Gospel,' and all that nauseous stuff? And what would be the verdict, in this suburban world, on a man who took no thought for the morrow, who regulated his life by the example of the lilies, who scoffed at the idea of saving money? You know perfectly well that his relations would have him declared a lunatic. *There* is the villainy. If you are continually professing an idolatrous and unctuous devotion to a body of teaching which you are also persistently and perpetually disregarding and disobeying in its plainest, most simple, most elementary injunctions, well, you will soon interest anglers in search of bait.

"Yes, such is the world behind the india-rubber plant into which Nelly entered. I believe she repelled the advances of 'master' with success. Her final undoing came from a different quarter, and I am afraid that drugs, not Biblical cajoleries, were the instruments used. She cried bitterly when she spoke of this event, but she said, too; 'I will kill him for it!' It was an ugly story, and a sad one, alas! - the saddest tale I ever listened to. Think of it: to come from that old cabin on the wild, bare hills, from the sound of the great sea, from the pure breath of the waves and the wet salt wind, to the stenches and the poisons of our 'industrial centres.' She came from parents who had nothing and possessed all things, to our civilisation which has everything, and lies on the dung-heap that it has made at the very gates of Heaven - destitute of all true treasures, full of sores and vermin and corruption. She was nurtured on the wonderful old legends of the saints and the fairies; she had listened to the songs that her father made and cut in Oghams; and we gave her the penny novelette and the works of Madame Chose. She had knelt before the altar, adoring the most holy sacrifice of the Mass; now she knelt beside 'master' while he approached the Lord in prayer, licking his fat white lips. I can imagine no more terrible transition.

"I do not know how or why it happened, but as I listened to Nelly's tale my eyes were opened to my own work and my own deeds, and I saw for the first time my wickedness. I should despair of explaining to anyone how utterly innocent I had been in intention all the while, how far I was from any deliberate design of guilt. In a sense, I was learned, and yet, in a sense, I was most ignorant; I had been committing what is, doubtless a grievous sin, under the impression that I was enjoying the greatest of all mysteries and graces and blessings - the great natural sacrament of human life.

"Did I not know I was doing wrong? I knew that if any of the masters found me with Nelly I should get into sad trouble. Certainly I knew that. But if any of the masters had caught me smoking a cigarette, or saying 'damn,' or going into a public-house to get a glass of beer, or using a crib, or reading Rabelais, I should have got into sad trouble also. I knew that I was sinning against the 'tone' of the great Public School; you may imagine how deeply I felt the guilt of such an offence as that! And, of course, I had heard the boys telling their foolish indecencies; but somehow their nasty talk and their filthy jokes were not in any way connected in my mind with my love of Nelly - no more, indeed, than midnight darkness suggests daylight, or torment symbolises pleasure. Indeed, there was a hint - a dim intuition - deep down in my consciousness that all was not well; but I knew of no reason for this; I held it a morbid dream, the fantasy of an imagination over-exalted, perhaps; I would not listen to a faint voice that seemed without sense or argument.

"And now that voice was ringing in my ears with the clear, resonant and piercing summons of a trumpet; I saw myself arraigned far down beside the pestilent horde of whom I have just spoken; and, indeed, my sin was worse than theirs, for I had been bred in light, and they in darkness. All heedless, without knowledge, without preparation, without receiving the mystic word, I had stumbled into the shrine, uninitiated I had passed beyond the veil and gazed upon the hidden mystery, on the secret glory that is concealed from the holy angels. Woe and great sorrow were upon me, as if a priest, devoutly offering the sacrifice, were suddenly to become aware that he was uttering, all inadvertently, hideous and profane blasphemies, summoning Satan in place of the Holy Spirit. I hid my face in my hands and cried out in my anguish.

"Do you know that I think Nelly was in a sense relieved when I tried to tell her of my mistake, as I called it; even though I said, as gently as I could, that it was all over. She was relieved, because for the first time she felt quite sure that I was altogether in my senses; I can understand it. My whole attitude must have struck her as bordering on insanity, for, of course, from first to last I had never for a moment taken up the position of the unrepentant but cheerful sinner, who knows that he is being a sad dog, but means to continue in his naughty way. She, with her evil experience, had thought the words I had sometimes uttered not remote from madness. She wondered, she told me, whether one night I might not suddenly take her throat in my hands and strangle her in a sudden frenzy. She hardly knew whether she dreaded such a death or longed for it.

"'You spoke so strangely,' she said; 'and all the while I knew we were doing wrong, and I wondered.'

"Of course, even after I had explained the matter as well as I could she was left to a large extent bewildered as to what my state of mind could have been; still, she saw that I was not mad, and she was relieved, as I have said.

"I do not know how she was first drawn to me - how it was that she stole that night to the room where I lay bruised and aching. Pity and desire and revenge, I suppose, all had their share. She was so sorry, she said, for me. She could see how lonely I was, how I hated the place and everybody about it, and she knew that I was not English. I think my wild Welsh face attracted her, too.

"Alas! that was a sad night, after all our laughter. We had sat on and on till the dawn began to come in through the drawn blinds. I told her that we must go to bed, or we should never get up the next day. We went into the bedroom, and there, sad and grey, the dawn appeared. There was a heavy sky covered with clouds and a straight, soft rain was pattering on the leaves of a great plane tree opposite; heavy drops fell into the pools in the road.

"It was still as on the mountain, filled with infinite sadness, and a sudden step clattering on the pavement of the square beyond made the stillness seem all the more profound. I stood by the window and gazed out at the weeping, dripping tree, the ever-falling rain and the motionless, leaden clouds - there was no breath of wind - and it was as if I heard the saddest of all music, tones of anguish and despair and notes that cried and wept. The theme was given out, itself wet, as it were, with tears. It was repeated with a sharper cry, a more piteous supplication; it was re-echoed with a bitter utterance, and tears fell faster as the raindrops fell plashing from the weeping tree. Inexorable in its sad reiterations, in its remorseless development, that music wailed and grew in its lamentation in my own heart; heavy it was, and without hope; heavy as those still, leaden clouds that hung motionless in heaven. No relief came to this sorrowing melody - rather a sharper note of anguish; and then for a moment, as if to embitter bitterness, sounded a fantastic, laughing air, a measure of jocund pipes and rushing violins, echoing with the mirth of dancing feet. But it was beaten into dust by the sentence of despair, by doom that was for ever, by a sentence pitiless, relentless; and, as a sudden breath shook the wet boughs of the plane tree and a torrent fell upon the road, so the last notes of that inner music were to me as a burst of hopeless weeping.

"I turned away from the window and looked at the dingy little room where we had laughed so well. It was a sad room enough, with its pale blue, stripy-patterned paper, its rickety old furniture and its feeble pictures. The only note of gaiety was on the dressing-table, where poor little Nelly had arranged some toys and trinkets and fantasies that she had bought for herself in the last few days. There was a silver-handled brush and a flagon of some scent that I liked, and a little brooch of olivines that had caught her fancy; and a powder-puff in a pretty gilt box. The sight of these foolish things cut me to the heart. But Nelly! She was standing by the bedside, half undressed, and she looked at me with the most piteous longing. I think that she had really grown fond of me. I suppose that I shall never forget the sad enchantment of her face, the flowing of her beautiful coppery hair about it; and the tears were wet on her cheeks. She half stretched out her bare arms to me and then let them fall. I had never known all her strange allurement before. I had refined and symbolised and made her into a sign of joy, and now before me she shone disarrayed - not a symbol, but a woman, in the new intelligence that had come to me, and I longed for her. I had just enough strength and no more."

EPILOGUE

It is unfortunate - or fortunate: that is a matter to be settled by the taste of the reader - that with this episode of the visit to London all detailed material for the life of Ambrose Meyrick comes to an end. Odd scraps of information, stray notes and jottings are all that is available, and the rest of Meyrick's life must be left in dim and somewhat legendary outline.

Personally, I think that this failure of documents is to be lamented. The four preceding chapters have, in the main, dealt with the years of boyhood, and therefore with a multitude of follies. One is inclined to wonder, as poor Nelly wondered, whether the lad was quite right in his head. It is possible that if we had fuller information as to his later years we might be able to dismiss him as decidedly eccentric, but well-meaning on the whole.

But, after all, I cannot be confident that he would get off so easily. Certainly he did not repeat the adventure of Little Russell Row, nor, so far as I am aware, did he address anyone besides his old schoolmaster in a Rabelaisian epistle. There are certain acts of lunacy which are like certain acts of heroism: they are hardly to be achieved twice by the same men.

But Meyrick continued to do odd things. He became a strolling player instead of becoming a scholar of Balliol. If he had proceeded to the University, he would have encountered the formative and salutary influence of Jowett. He wandered up and down the country for two or three years with the actors, and writes the following apostrophe to the memory of his old company.

"I take off my hat when I hear the old music, for I think of the old friends and the old days; of the theatre in the meadows by the sacred river, and the swelling song of the nightingales on sweet, spring nights. There is no doubt that we may safely hold with Plato his opinion, and safely may we believe that all brave earthly shows are but broken copies and dim lineaments of immortal things. Therefore, I hope and trust that I shall again be gathered unto the true Hathaway Company *quæ sursum est*, which is the purged and exalted image of the lower, which plays for ever a great mystery in the theatre of the meadows of asphodel, which wanders by the happy, shining streams, and drinks from an Eternal Cup in a high and blissful and everlasting Tavern. *Ave, cara sodalitas, ave semper.*"

Thus does he translate into wild speech *crêpe* hair and grease paints, dirty dressing-rooms and dirtier lodgings. And when his strolling days were over he settled down in London, paying occasional visits to his old home in the west. He wrote three or four books which are curious and interesting in their way, though they will never be popular. And finally he went on a strange errand to the East; and from the East there was for him no returning.

It will be remembered that he speaks of a Celtic cup, which had been preserved in one family for many hundred years. On the death of the last "Keeper" this cup was placed in Meyrick's charge. He received it with the condition that it was to be taken to a certain concealed shrine in Asia and there deposited in hands that would know how to hide its glories for ever from the evil world.

He went on this journey into unknown regions, travelling by ragged roads and mountain passes, by the sandy wilderness and the mighty river. And he forded his way by the quaking and dubious track that winds in and out among the dangers and desolations of the *Kevir* - the great salt slough.

He came at last to the place appointed and gave the word and the treasure to those who know how to wear a mask and to keep well the things which are committed to them, and then set out on his journey back. He had reached a point not very far from the gates of West and halted for a day or two amongst Christians, being tired out with a weary pilgrimage. But the Turks or the Kurds - it does not matter which - descended on the place and worked their customary works, and so Ambrose was taken by them.

One of the native Christians, who had hidden himself from the miscreants, told afterwards how he saw "the stranger Ambrosian" brought out, and how they held before him the image of the Crucified that he might spit upon it and trample it under his feet. But he kissed the icon with great joy and penitence and devotion. So they bore him to a tree outside the village and crucified him there.

And after he had hung on the tree some hours, the infidels, enraged, as it is said, by the shining rapture of his face, killed him with their spears.

It was in this manner that Ambrose Meyrick gained Red Martyrdom and achieved the most glorious Quest and Adventure of the Sangraal.

THE END

NOTES

1. A highly Rabelaisian phrase is omitted.

2. Translated from the Welsh verses quoted in the notebook.

3. The following translation of these verses appeared in *Poems from the Old Bards*, by Taliesin, Bristol, 1812:

> *"In Soar's sweet valley, where the sound*
> *Of holy anthems once was heard*
> *From many a saint, the hills prolong*
> *Only the music of the bird.*
>
> *In Soar's sweet valley, where the brook*
> *With many a ripple flows along,*
> *Delicious prospects meet the eye,*
> *The ear is charmed with Phil'mel's song.*
>
> *In Soar's sweet valley once a Maid,*
> *Despising worldly prospects gay,*
> *Resigned her note in earthly choirs*
> *Which now in Heaven must sound alway.*
>
> *In Soar's sweet valley David preached;*
> *Gospel accents so beguiled*
> *The savage Britons, that they turned*
> *Their fiercest cries to music mild.*
>
> *In Soar's sweet valley Cybi taught*
> *To haughty Prince the Holy Law,*
> *The way to Heaven he showed, and then*
> *The subject tribes inspired with awe.*
>
> *In Soar's sweet valley still the song*
> *Of Phil'mel sounds and checks alarms.*
> *But when shall I once more renew*
> *Those heavenly hours in Gladys' arms?"*

"Taliesin" was the pseudonym of an amiable clergyman, the Reverend Owen Thomas, for many years curate of Llantrisant. He died in 1820, at the great age of eighty-four. His original poetry in Welsh was reputed as far superior to his translations, and he made a very valuable and curious collection of "Cymric Antiquities," which remains in manuscript in the keeping of his descendants.

Parchment Books is committed to publishing high quality
Esoteric/Occult classic texts at a reasonable price.

With the premium on space in modern dwellings, we also strive - within the limits of good book design - to make our products as slender as possible, allowing more books to be fitted into a given bookshelf area.

Parchment Books is an imprint of Aziloth Books, which has established itself as a publisher boasting a diverse list of powerful, quality titles, including novels of flair and originality, and factual publications on controversial issues that have not found a home in the rather staid and politically-correct atmosphere of many publishing houses.

Titles Include:

Psychic Self-Defence	Dion Fortune
The Ancient Wisdom	Annie Besant
The Masters and the Path	C W Leadbeater
Man, His True Nature & Ministry	Louis-Claude de St.-Martin
Secret Doctrines of the Rosicrucians	Magus Incognito
Corpus Hermeticum	(trans. GRS Mead)
The Virgin of the World	Hermes Trismegistus
Raja Yoga	Yogi Ramacharaka
Theosophy	Rudolf Steiner
The Interior Castle	St Teresa of Avila
The Gospel of Thomas	Anonymous
Pistis Sophia	(trans. GRS Mead)
The Signature of All Things	Jacob Boehme
The Secret Destiny of America	Manly P Hall
Practical Mysticism	Evelyn Underhill
The Rosicrucian Mysteries	Max Heindel
The Conference of Birds	Farid ud-Din Attar
Meetings With Remarkable Men	G I Gurdjieff
The Everlasting Man	G K Chesterton
The Voice of the Silence	H P Blavatsky
War Is A Racket	Maj.-General Smedley D. Butler

Obtainable at all good online and local bookstores.

View Parchment Books' full list at: www.azilothbooks.com
We are a small, approachable company and would love to hear any of your comments and suggestions on our plans, products, or indeed on absolutely anything. Aziloth is also interested in hearing from aspiring authors whom we might publish. We look forward to meeting you. Contact us at:

info@azilothbooks.com.

CATHEDRAL CLASSICS

Parchment Book's sister imprint, Cathedral Classics, hosts an array of classic literature, from ancient tomes to twentieth-century masterpieces, all of which deserve a place in your home. A small selection is detailed below:

Mary Shelley	*Frankenstein*
H G Wells	*The Time Machine; The Invisible Man*
Niccolo Machiavelli	*The Prince*
Omar Khayyam	*The Rubaiyat of Omar Khayyam*
Joseph Conrad	*Heart of Darkness; The Secret Agent*
Jane Austen	*Persuasion; Northanger Abbey*
Oscar Wilde	*The Picture of Dorian Gray*
Voltaire	*Candide*
Bulwer Lytton	*The Coming Race*
Arthur Conan Doyle	*The Adventures of Sherlock Holmes*
John Buchan	*The Thirty-Nine Steps*
Friedrich Nietzsche	*Beyond Good and Evil*
George Eliot	*Silas Marner*
Henry James	*Washington Square*
Stephen Crane	*The Red Badge of Courage*
Ralph Waldo Emmerson	*Self-Reliance, and Other Essays, (series 1&2)*
Sun Tzu	*The Art of War*
Charles Dickens	*A Christmas Carol*
Fyodor Dostoyevsky	*The Gambler; The Double*
Virginia Wolf	*To the Lighthouse; Mrs Dalloway.*
Johann W Goethe	*The Sorrows of Young Werther*
Walt Whitman	*Leaves of Grass - 1855 edition*
Confucius	*Analects*
Anonymous	*Beowulf*
Anne Bronte	*Agnes Grey*
More	*Utopia*
Farid ud-Din Attar	*The Conference of Birds*
Jack London	*Call of the Wild*
Edwin A. Abbott	*Flatland*

full list at: www.azilothbooks.com

Obtainable at all good online and local bookstores.

THE CARTON CHRONICLES

THE CURIOUS TALE OF
FLASHMAN'S TRUE FATHER

Keith Laidler

Morose, cynical and given to drink, Sydney Carton is one of Charles Dickens' most famous characters; a cold, dispassionate man, yet capable, in the final moments of A Tale of Two Cities, of sacrificing himself beneath the guillotine for Lucie, the woman he both loved and lost.

It now appears, however, that Dickens was being somewhat economical with the *actualité.*

Newly recovered documents, written in Carton's own hand, tell a far different tale. Sydney Carton survived his execution, only to find himself at the mercy of the monstrous Robespierre, author of the Paris Terror. His love Lucie languishes in a French prison, her husband dead, and Carton can ensure her survival only by becoming Robespierre's personal spy.

Reluctant, terrified and often drunk, Carton blunders his way through the major events of the French Revolution, grudgingly partaking in some of the blackest deeds of the Terror and, by a mixture of cowardice, bravado and luck, lending a hand in the fall of most of its leading figures. Kidnapped by the British, he finds himself a double agent, trusted by neither side. Our hero chronicles the slow decay of revolutionary ideals and, in passing, casts light on the true parentage of that sadistic villain of "Tom Brown's Schooldays", the beastly Flashman.

Praise for Keith Laidler's writing:

*"Laidler's book is meticulously researched and covers
a fascinating period"* (The Times)

"It is a riveting story, and Laidler tells it well" (Telegraph Review)

From all good online and local bookstores.